BELIEVE IN WONDER

CREDO IN STUPOREM

BOOK 1 OF MYSTERIES OF THE LAUREL SOCIETY

THE WONDEROUS SCIENCE

BRIAN & JOSIE PARKER

BELIEVE IN WONDER PUBLISHING

PORTLAND • OREGON

"*Wonder is the beginning of wisdom.*"

- Socrates

Edited by Rachel Lulich of Broken Top Editing

Book designed and illustration by Brian W. Parker, BFA, MA
Inside text set in Baskerville, Adobe Caslon, and Felix Titling MT
BIW "reading boy" logo is a trademark of Believe In Wonder Publishing, LLC

Printed in the U.S.A
For bulk orders, event booking, and questions about publishing services,
please email us at believeinwonderpublishing@gmail.com

ISBN-13: 978-1542680530
ISBN-10: 9781542680530

First Edition (revised)

Summary: Follow the adventures of Zora Sparks, her brother Nathan, and enigmatic
Ms. Daisy Kidd as they delve into the magic and mysteries of The Laurel Society.

Believe In Wonder is a family-owned, youth focused publishing company based in Portland, OR.
We delight in promoting imagination, inspiration, and positive thinking in kids and adults alike,
and strive to bring diverse characters and new worlds to readers and art lovers everywhere.

Visit us at **believeinwonder.com** for more books, art, and event updates.

THE WONDEROUS SCIENCE

BRIAN & JOSIE PARKER

for Victor

always have the courage
to strive for your dreams

CONTENTS

PROLOGUE: DARK CORNERS

In the deep shadows of the crypt, amidst the whirling eddies of dry leaves and sweeps of spiderwebs, someone stirred. He nervously slid his Italian leather shoe back and forth across the wet stones. Twilight was slowly turning to true night and a downy cloak of mist was cast over the field of headstones. Sirens wailed a few blocks away, accompanied by the slow tap-tap-tap of rain water falling from the corner of the moss covered mausoleums. Two figures now shifted in the gloom, pulling up the collars of their jackets. One was tall and broad, while the other had a thin build and wore wire-framed glasses that caught the light with each quick glance at his watch.

"Fifteen minutes late. Hopefully there wasn't a problem," the thin man said.

Suddenly, a glow blossomed out of the murk, like the soft twinkle of Christmas lights in the distance. Another figure appeared before them, landing gracefully on the marble steps of the crypt, heels clicking on the stone. The new arrival stood straight and primly tipped her hat.

"Sorry for my tardiness –" she said but was stopped short by the thin man.

"Please, my dear, let us use the names we have chosen," he said in a whisper. " We never know who is watching."

"Of course, Mr. Nail," she replied, nodding to the thin man, "and Mr. Hammer," nodding to the tall, broad one.

"Thank you, Ms. Razor, and never mind the lateness. It doesn't matter as long as you obtained what I requested." Mr. Nail spoke in a quiet, confident tone, but underneath this veneer, there was an edge and a sense of impatience as he adjusted his glasses. He stepped forward a bit in the shadows, remaining concealed, and extended his gloved hand. When Ms. Razor pulled the brown parcel from her coat, he snatched it away and rushed to open it, tossing the wrappings unceremoniously to the ground. Inside the now ruined package sat three large gears, each covered in intricate engravings. He smiled and carefully turned each one in his hands and examined the archaic symbols, admiring the shiny surface as they caught the distant light of the city. "Excellent! You've done well. We are only missing one now. The crucial component." He quickly pocketed the gears and turned to leave, but Ms. Razor reached out to stop him.

"Wait. Don't you want an update on the…other issue?" she said. "I thought the girl was important to the plan."

Mr. Nail's eyes gleamed just over the rim of his glasses, cold and disquieting, that seemed to steal the very warmth from the air.

"The girl is imperative to the plan," he replied in a hushed voice. "But never fear Ms. Razor – I have kept a close eye on her. She'll be ready when the time is right. I've seen how this all plays out, remember." He tapped the edge of his wire-framed spectacles and smiled.

When he turned away this time, he laid his hand on Mr. Hammer's shoulder, and in a brilliant flash of light they were gone, leaving Ms. Razor alone, shrouded in the gray mist.

Zora was having nightmares again. They had been getting worse since she and her brother had moved in at 1515 Anders Place. She was rolling back and forth in her bed, sweat beading on her forehead when a hand came out of the darkness and pulled her awake.

"AHHH!" she screamed, and reached for the bat she kept at her bedside before realizing it was only Nate, now staring back at her wide-eyed in the bluish dark of her room.

"JEZZ ZORA! Calm down, will ya!" He had covered his head, awaiting a blow that never came. "Could you please dial down the crazy for a sec?"

"What are you doing in here, Nate?" Zora sat upright and tried to rub the sleep out her eyes. Her thick hair stood straight up, as per usual, but now there was a sock hanging just above her eye which she grumpily snatched away.

"I was watching you wrestle with your sheets and drool all over the place, of course."

"Seriously. It's like 3:00 in the morning. Teresa is gonna go fireball if she sees you wandering around."

Nate crossed his arms indignantly. "I'm not wandering around. You told me to let you know if anything happened with your little project."

"And?"

"Well, you'd better come with me."

Zora and Nate moved slowly down the hall passed Teresa's door and into Nate's cluttered room. Toys lay strewn across the floor like some kind of fantasy battlefield, soldiers holding tightly to their weapons in the dim light.

"Ouch!" Zora's foot found a pile of camouflaged Legos near the bed, and she jumped away, stifling curses.

"Sorry," Nate said, "forgot to remind you of the booby traps." He quickly retrieved a small, dark box from under his mattress. "Here, it won't stop humming."

Zora took the box. She too felt the strange humming emanating from within. She opened it and reached inside to run her finger over the scroll worked surface, but the second her hand touched the object it began to glow softly with golden light. She and Nate looked on in wonder.

"Wow," her brother said, moving in close for a better look. "It's never done that before."

Zora pushed Nate's large head out of the way. "Of course it hasn't. Something has changed." She examined it closer but saw nothing different about the object save for the new glow. "Maybe something is affecting it."

"Like what, Zo?"

Zora removed the small brass gear from the box and held it close to her face. A smile creased her nose, and her eyes shimmered. "I don't know, Nate. I really don't know."

THE ABYSMAL NANNY

Daisy Kidd scooped the last bits of cake out of her eyes, removed her bowler hat, and sat down hard on the patio steps. "Ok. I'll say it. My magic sucks," she said to herself and surveyed the disaster before her.

The birthday party had gone far worse than she had hoped. The garden and backyard belonging to her employers, Dr. John and Mary Martin and their nine-year-old twins, was now covered in a six-inch thick coating of birthday cake shrapnel. The twenty other children in attendance were now running, sliding, fighting, and crying in a blizzard of marzipan, frosting, and sprinkles. The twins stood in the middle of it all – their expensive pink party dresses obscured by massive chunks of dessert. As they came stomping, along with their parents, through the sugary apocalypse, Daisy could tell this most recent attempt at using her powers had failed to impress them.

"DAISY! This is a CATASTROPHE!" the girls screamed in unison, crossing their sticky arms. "You said this party was going to be magical! You said this party was going to be incredible! You said–!"

"I know, I know! Keep your pants on!" Daisy replied, a forced smile creasing her freckled nose. She held up her hands in defense. "Obviously things didn't go quite the way I had planned."

In truth, she didn't have a clue what had gone wrong. Maybe she messed up the calibrations on the Perkins Cake-Topper, or maybe the Louis Anti-Gravinator had malfunctioned, but she quickly remembered one of the first lines from her Warden's Handbook: Only a poor Warden blames their instruments. Whatever had happened, she was to blame and she was the one looking like a fool.

"Ms. Kidd, you came to us from a very reputable agency! I knew taking on a seventeen-year-old nanny was a mistake!" Mrs. Martin growled.

"I'm almost eighteen," Daisy said under her breath.

"It doesn't matter! Despite your age, you are supposed to be a professional!" Dr. Martin said, his face red (and slightly sprinkled). He pointed towards his pool, which had inexplicably turned into berry blue Jell-O. "This kind of thing looks very UNprofessional! I hope this is the last of your 'surprises.'"

"Oh jeez! I forgot about the pool." Daisy composed herself, primly brushing some frosting from her red curls. "If you give me a couple of minutes, we can set this all right. Really." She spoke through gritted teeth, but her large green eyes had a hint of pleading in them. "Stephanie will be here any minute. She's the best."

Almost on cue, Daisy felt a slight shift in the air. From the corner of her eye, she saw her friend appear out of the clear blue sky, her long golden hair flowing in an unseen wind. When she landed on the far side of the yard, the soft aura of light around her dissipated, and she straightened her skirt and tucked her umbrella neatly under her arm. None of the other party goers noticed her arrival, but non-practitioners very rarely noticed the use of the Wonderous Science. That is unless you wanted them to – or you blew up a cake right in front of them.

As she approached, Stephanie Love put on a smile that radiated confidence and authority. "Mr. and Mrs. Martin I presume," she said very properly. "It is a pleasure to meet you. Daisy has said such nice things about–"

The twins stopped her short. "She said you could fix this!" they screamed.

"Pipe down you horrible little…!" Daisy said through gritted teeth. She had just about enough at this point, but luckily Stephanie quickly stepped in between her and the twins.

"That I shall. Please, will all of you go attend to the party guests and we'll have this mess cleaned up in two shakes."

The Martins walked away in a huff, and Stephanie sat down beside Daisy and crossed her legs.

"Are you alright?"

"Yeah, except for the fact that my goose is completely and thoroughly cooked! I've done it now. I'm going to be demoted for sure this time." Daisy let out a long sigh of defeat. "And I did everything right, I'm sure of it."

"Well, it's not so bad. A little exploded cake, some transmuted pool water. All in all, not a complete catastrophe."

Suddenly, a look of dazed horror washed over Daisy's face.

"There might be one more tiny problem," she whispered.

"What?"

"Welllll…I used the Super-Animator and…"

Just as Daisy was trying to explain, Stephanie's eye was drawn away and she could see the "tiny problem" for herself. The door to the shed across the yard burst open, and a cavalcade of prancing pink pinatas came stampeding into the party – bleating, huffing, and howling "CANDY!" at the top of their paper mache lungs. Daisy sat frozen as the pink ponies romped into the party chaos, wondering why she'd gone with a pony theme.

"Look out!" she cried, but it was too late, and soon the children were charging all over the back yard, most screaming with joy as they were covered by the rainbow-colored wave.

Stephanie pulled a small compact from her handbag, flipped it open, and breathed onto the mirror inside, which changed instantly from her own reflection to that of a grizzled old man with a thick gray mustache and small, intense eyes.

"Mr. Porter, we have a Level 3 magical event at 251 Hollycrest!" she said urgently, then turned to Daisy. "Get your things, we're leaving." Daisy grabbed her hat and was quickly dragged towards the gate.

"What's the situation?" said the grizzled man whose face had appeared in the mirror.

"Nothing to be too concerned over," Stephanie replied, "but please send Stewards immediately. We'll need memory wipes and clean-up."

"Isn't that Daisy's assignment?" he grumbled with a slightly Eastern accent. "That's not good. She's still on probation."

"Yes, Mr. Porter. But enough chatter, please. A fast resolution to this probem would be nice."

Stephanie straightened her bowler hat, buttoned up her coat, and prompted Daisy to do likewise.

"Shouldn't I say good-bye to the Martins?" Daisy asked, pulling her own hat down tight over her head, slightly obscuring her eyes with a mess of red curls.

"I'm sure they'll understand dear," Stephanie replied.

A soft twinkling of light surrounded her as she kicked off. They both lifted quickly from the ground, leaving the squeals of manic party glee behind them.

Daisy didn't like flying, not even in the best of circumstances. There just seemed to be too many variables – too much that could go wrong. The mechanism in her bowler hat had to be checked and calibrated, and the Feather-Light coat she wore couldn't have one tear or loose seam. Anything out of place meant falling from the sky. Bearing this in mind, she usually opted to travel like a regular person, but Stephanie always insisted that it was their duty to travel "as Wardens do." It didn't stop Daisy from holding on to her like her life depended on it as the city of Portland whooshed past her dangling feet, a river of blurred buildings, parks, and streets.

After the hasty exit from the party, there wasn't much discussion in flight, but Daisy knew something was wrong when they landed on Quimby Street near The Brown Bowler, a small coffee shop and ice cream parlor that practitioners frequented. Stephanie liked to bring her there when she wanted to soften the blow of bad news.

When they touched down on the sidewalk, Daisy's legs went all wobbly from the flight, and the delicate glow of magic dissipated into soft baubles of light. Stephanie took her arm as she stumbled unnoticed to the entrance of the cafe, the door bell jingling cheerfully as they walked into the cozy interior. It was a small place, filled with the comforting smells of brewed cappuccino and fresh cookies. The bistro style tables were polished to a high gloss, as always, reflecting the soft white lights strung along the walls.

"Hello ladies," said a mellow voice from behind the counter. "Take a seat. I'll be just a sec."

"Thanks, Rodney," Stephanie replied, and took a seat.

Daisy followed suit, happy to be off her feet, but caught a quick glimpse of her reflection off of the tabletop and realized that she still had cake on her from the explosion. Instinctively, she tapped the tip of her umbrella three times on the hardwood floor and closed her eyes. Within seconds, the sugary residue disappeared, pulled away by a sweep of light, leaving her face and uniform pristine.

"Nicely done," Stephanie said.

Daisy looked again at her reflection and smiled. Her red curls were back to their usual sheen, and her black pea coat and bowler had been thoroughly de-caked. The hat and coat were standard issue uniforms for field Wardens of The Laurel Society, but since Daisy never liked dressing in dark colors, she had decided to brighten up the ensemble with a tangerine scarf and red paisley skirt – definitely not standard issue. She stood in sharp contrast with other Wardens like Stephanie, who wore all black save for the freshly starched white blouse that peaked over the collar of their coats.

"Thanks, I guess," Daisy replied. "Simple wonders have always come easily to me. Cleaning spells and tools, cooking apparatus, finding, binding, you know – the little things. It's this big stuff, real wonderous tools, that always seems to blow up in my face."

"Or in other's faces," Stephanie added with a pert smile.

"Yeah. That too."

"Well, we're going to have to do something about that, aren't we?" Stephanie tossed her hair, and looked Daisy squarely in the eye. "We are part of a proud tradition, Daisy. For over two centuries, the Laurel Society has guided the destinies of those gifted in magic.

The Stewards, the Wardens, the Tinkers-Tailors, the Daggers, and the Watchers have brought about great change in the world, but it has always been the Warden's great responsibility to nurture young people with the potential to be practitioners of the Wonderous Science, and rear them for the great power they will someday wield."

Daisy couldn't help but to roll her eyes. "I know," she grumbled, "I've had this drilled into my head a hundred times already. The Wardens are tasked with protecting and inspiring magical potential," she recited, "and determining if they are a risk to themselves or others. It's all in the handbook!"

Stephanie cleared her throat, paused, and began again. "As I was saying, how can the Society expect you to take on that kind of responsibility if those twins were too much for you? They aren't even potentials, Daisy! As your sponsor, it falls to me to make sure you reach all of your qualifications before your probationary period is up. If not, you know what happens."

Daisy felt her shoulders slump at the thought of it. She had grown up in the Laurel Society, raised by a sixty-year member, and had dreamed of becoming a Warden since she was a little girl. They were the elite. After almost five years with the Stewards, the support division of the Society, this was her chance to prove she has what it takes. If she did not, then it was back to being a Steward – permanently.

"I can do this, Steph," she said. "I was born to do this. I just need a little more practice." By the sound of her voice, even Daisy wasn't sure she was telling the truth, but saying it out loud did make her feel a little better.

"For your sake, I hope you figure it all out soon."

A light began to emanate from Stephanie's handbag. She reached in and removed her compact, which was pulsating with a blue glow. Daisy got up so she could get a better look. When Stephanie opened it, Mr. Porter's face once again appeared.

"The situation at the Martin's house has been handled," he said in an even tone. Daisy had known Mr. Porter since she was three years old, and had never heard the man sound anything but calm and matter-of-fact.

"Thanks, Lou," she said, and gave him a little wave to which he smiled.

"My pleasure, love. Try to not blow up, melt down, or implode anything else this week, would you? I've got Stewards logging in overtime, and you know I don't like being wasteful."

"Will do."

"Is that all, Mr. Porter?" Stephanie asked impatiently.

"One more thing. The new Watcher arrived today, and a week ahead of schedule too. Been goin' through our books all day, him and his 'assistant.' He asked to see Daisy as soon as possible. From the looks of him, I don't think this guy likes to be kept waiting."

Mr. Porter's face faded away quickly, leaving Daisy and Stephanie's reflections looking a little shocked.

"Me! Why would he want to see me?"

"I haven't the slightest, dear."

Rodney walked over to their table and pulled out a pen and pad.

"So what would you ladies like? We have a special today on sherbets."

Barely seeing him, Daisy said, "Nothing for me, thanks. Suddenly I'm not in the mood." She stood and headed quickly for the door.

THE CHAPTER HOUSE

A few blocks from the cafe in the Alphabet District of Portland was a large house seated at the corner of Quimby and 24th. It sat high on a hill, surrounded by thick trees and a head-high iron fence made to look like the loops and swirls of laurel branches. It was almost impossible to see from the street, its white crown only visible over the tops of thinned poplar trees covered with the last of their autumn foliage, but she didn't need to see it to know that she was home.

Daisy had memorized every eave and shutter of the place. When she reached the gate, she tapped it gently with the small ring on her right hand. It too was shaped like laurel leaves, but made of silver. There was a pleasant clink, and the gate opened with the slightest squeak of its hinges. Past the hedges and up the hill, the house stood three stories tall, white with pistachio green shutters and surrounded by a well-tended lawn and garden. It was, by most standards, a nice but ordinary-looking house. Above it, Daisy could see the coming and going of other Wardens, landing on the roof or taking off for assignments in other parts of the city. This was the Portland Chapter House of the Laurel Society, Protectors of Magic and Practitioners of The Wonderous Science.

Daisy was greeted at the door by Mr. Porter, who immediately took her hat and coat with a broad smile behind his thick mustache. "You've had an interesting morning, Little Flower," he said with a wink.

"Interesting is one way of putting it. Thanks, Lou," she said hurriedly. Usually, she would have taken a minute to say hello, but she had pressing business to attend to.

"You're welcome, Ms. Kidd. You know where the main office is, so be off with you, and don't forget to sign in."

"I've got to see Aunt Mizzy first."

Mr. Porter's brow furrowed. "I hope you aren't planning on skipping your meeting…"

"No. I just have to see her. It's been days, and I have to make sure she's getting by ok without me."

"I understand. I've been looking after her at home, so don't worry yourself too much." Mr. Porter and her aunt lived miles away from the Chapter House in an interesting place called the Rookery, but she never missed afternoon tea here – after years of sticking to a strict schedule, Mildred Mizner was not one to change things up on a whim. Mr. Porter handed Daisy a knit blanket from the chair beside the door and waved her off towards the library. "Take her this, since you're headed that way, but don't be too long. I'm sure the new Watcher knows you're here already." He tapped the side of his nose and waved her on her way.

The house was massive on the inside – far larger than the exterior suggested, and the vertically striped walls were covered with portraits and artifacts from the Society's fabled past, each room more amazing and bizarre than the one before it. Daisy walked briskly into the grand entryway and was quickly caught up in the bustle of her fellow Wardens checking in from all over the city, each in their regulation pea coat and bowler hat. In the center of the space stood a marble podium, on which sat a leather bound ledger that every Warden stopped by to sign.

"Hi Daisy!" Audrey Lane, another Warden in Daisy's group, greeted her with a firm slap on the back. "How is your first week working out?"

"I'd better not say," she replied, quickly signing her name to the ledger. Audrey always came off a little smug, and with the day she was having, Daisy wasn't in the mood to explain her recent failures.

"I get it. Kids right? My first charges were the worst. Triplets with no talents whatsoever, and on top of that they always smelled like sausage for some reason. It gets better, though."

"I appreciate the encouragement," Daisy replied, sidestepping her and moving on into the hall to find her aunt.

Daisy had only been a member of the Wardens for a few months, and after her training, she was hoping to find herself doing a lot better. She had been raised around magic her whole life and had been a member of the Stewards division for a year. Stewards were tasked with detecting rogue magic, wild magic, and misuses of the Wonderous Science – basically, they were the clean-up crew. Daisy didn't mind the work, and Mr. Porter had been a pretty great boss, but she had always dreamed of being a Warden. To inspire a new generation of practitioners of the Wonderous Science was a big responsibility and one that she took seriously, even if her results suggested otherwise.

Daisy pushed open the double doors leading into the library and took in a deep, comforting breath. This had always been her favorite part of the house, and she had spent hours there as a child flipping through giant map books or building table forts with the antique mahogany furniture. It was the smell that she loved – the smell of old leather-bound books, and of wood polish, and brass cleaner. Something about it spoke to her soul, conjuring images of adventures in far-off places. Amongst the tall shelves was a sitting area near the far wall with plush red velvet armchairs looking out on the gardens. There, seated next to an open window, was her Aunt Mizzy.

"It's about time you brought that blanket," she said softly and continued reading, running her soft, dark hands along the impressed pages of the book in her lap. "Come on over and give you aunty some sugar, girl."

Daisy happily did as instructed. She kissed her aunt on the cheek, laying the blanket over her legs, then took a seat beside her. The old woman never looked her way, but a quiet smile appeared wrinkling the brown skin at the corners of her pale eyes. Ms. Mizner was not really Daisy's aunt. They had not a drop of common blood between them, but they were a family all the same. She had known Daisy's parents for many years, and when they passed she took her in and raised her as her own. With her position in the Laurel Society, no one ever dared argued the point.

"So, how are things going with your assignment?" Aunt Mizzy said. She closed her book and waited patiently for an answer.

"Do you really need to ask? Haven't you seen it already?"

"Yes I have, but I wanted to be polite," she replied. Aunt Mizzy pushed the peculiar spectacles she wore upon her nose and the lenses flashed for a split second with a brilliant sheen of colors, then returned to their original dark tint.

"Well, a lot of words come to mind, but disaster and failure are at the top of the list."

"That's unfortunate. Well, you'll never learn anything if you're afraid to blow something up!" she laughed, snickered and snorted. Daisy was less amused.

"You could have given me a heads up, you know," she pouted. "What's the point of having an aunt who can see the future if she's not willing to throw you some hints every now and again."

"Sorry, no freebies. You know that's not how I play things. You need to experience life as it happens, just like everybody else. That's the only way you grow." She pulled the blanket up over her lap and snuggled deeper into the plush armchair. "Besides, my visions aren't what they used to be."

Aunt Mizzy smiled coyly like she was prone to do, and Daisy wondered how true that statement really was. Her aunt was as crafty as they come, and after ninety-five years, sixty of which were spent as head Watcher and director of the chapter house, she knew how to play her cards close to the vest. The Watchers' gift was different from any of the other Wonderous Sciences – they could divine the future with the use of specially crafted lenses. The stronger the gift, the clearer the visions. Although Mrs. Mizner had been mostly blind since birth, she was considered to be one of the best, and Daisy was sure that retirement hadn't dulled any of her senses or her razor sharp tongue for that matter.

"I'm supposed to go see the new Watcher today," Daisy mumbled. "Right now, in fact. I don't know what it's all about, but I'm sure it has to do with my Warden status. I don't suspect this would be the one time you would break your rule?" She asked, knowing full well that her aunt was set on the matter. Strangely enough, Aunt Mizzy's smile faded and she turned to Daisy with a look of concern.

"Things are about to change, little flower," she whispered. There was a sober weight to each word she spoke, like the sound of a base drum. "But don't be afraid. Things always change, and I know you can rise to the occasion." She reached out her hands and Daisy took them in her own.

"Wow. Way to go, Aunt Mizzy. Now I'm freaking out." Daisy squeezed her hands gently. "Anything else you got for me? I like some sweet with my portents of doom."

"You are going to make some new friends. How's that?"

"Better, I guess."

"Good. Now get ready, your meeting is about to begin."

Just then, the door to the library opened and in walked a large man. He stood almost seven feet tall, with a gleaming bald head and impossibly square jaw. He wore a dark suit and gray vest that only brought attention to his immaculately white gloves. As he walked towards them, Daisy couldn't help but notice the way he moved – graceful for a man his size and strangely like a large jungle cat stalking through tall grass. He stopped at the chair and stood with his arms behind his back.

"Ms. Daisy Kidd," he said, more statement than a question.

"Yes. Unfortunately, that's me," Daisy replied with a nervous chuckle. "I don't think we've had the pleasure?"

"I'm Hobbs," he said flatly. "Just Hobbs. You're late for you meeting. I was sent to get you."

"She was just leaving, Hobbs," Aunt Mizzy said, and patted Daisy on the knee. "Go on dear. We'll talk later."

As Daisy got up to leave, Mizzy placed a folded piece of paper in her hand. Before she could ask what it was, Mizzy said, "Open it after your meeting, and remember what we talked about, ok?"

"Yes Ma'am," she replied and followed Hobbs' broad shoulders out of the library.

The director's office was in the east wing of the house, up the grand staircase and past the offices of the Stewards' division where Daisy used to work. There were fewer windows on that side of the house, for some odd reason or another, and the yellow light coming from the Tiffany lamps cast strange shadows across the walls. At the end of a long hallway, decorated on both sides with tall portraits of former directors, was a large door with a brass plaque in its center. It read,

"We are the tinkers of enlightenment,
the stewards of the power,
the wardens to protect the weak,
the watchers on the tower,
the daggers to snuff out the cruel,
and the hands that raise up kings,
unshroud the light so wonderous,
and to you, our voices sing."

Daisy had read the words a hundred times before, and could recite them with her eyes closed – but then again, every member of the Society could.

Hobbs opened the door and escorted her inside. Even though this had been her aunt's office for many years, she barely recognized it now. Gone were all of the photos and mementos of Ms. Mizner's days as the director, along with the worn furniture and bizarre artifacts she had accumulated in her time there. A lot of people had thought Ms. Mizner was a bit of pack rat, hoarding every piece of correspondence or wonderous implement she had ever received, but Daisy had always liked the clutter. Her aunt had called it "evidence of genius," which always made Daisy laugh. She'd never been one for false humility.

The room was now cleared, and the furniture replaced with dark leather chairs, angular black tables and shelves, and cold steel picture frames filled with the kind of art you might see in a hotel lobby. Even the old Persian rugs had been replaced with beige carpet which looked to Daisy like a small sea of tapioca pudding. Sitting in the middle of the unnerving order of it all was a massive black desk, behind which sat a rail-thin man in a black suit and gray waistcoat. He stood as she entered and extended his hand.

"Please take a seat, Ms. Kidd," he said, taking her hand firmly in his own and motioning towards an empty chair. "My name is Arthur Flint – you may call me Mr. Flint. It is very nice to meet you." He spoke with a crisp sort of accent that Daisy couldn't quite place, and everything about the man appeared to be pressed and starched, from the perfect part in his hair to his thin lips and mustache. His spectacles were wire framed with side shields containing small clockwork gears. The lenses were dark but had a rainbow sheen when they caught the light – just like the pair Aunt Mizzy wore.

"Nice to meet you as well," she said shyly and took the seat provided.

"That will be all, Hobbs," Flint said. He was making notes in a large ledger and waved Hobbs out distractedly. "Please let me know when the final package arrives. The one we discussed." Hobbs nodded and backed out of the door, keeping a hard eye on Daisy all the way until the latch clicked.

"He's an…interesting guy, isn't he?" Daisy said with a grin.

"I'm sure he is. Hobbs is my assistant, but we rarely talk about personal matters. Have you ever met a Dagger before, Ms. Kidd?"

"Never here!" she blurted out. "We've never had a Dagger division in Portland, not that I remember anyway, but I guess you know that being the new director and all." She was smiling awkwardly, but couldn't seem to make herself stop, and her palms were sweating so much that she kept rubbing them against her skirt. "Aunt Mizzy use to tell me about them, and one time she took me with her on a trip to Chicago and I met one. I think his name was Mr. Thrash, or Snatch, or something just as unnerving."

"Well, you'll be seeing more of them," Mr. Flint said. "Along with Hobbs, I will have another five stationed here in the coming week."

"Wow, six Daggers! When did we get so popular?" she chuckled. Mr. Flint looked up, completely unamused.

"As of right now, I'm afraid," he said quite seriously and set his pen and ledger aside. "Things have become difficult for us in recent months, Ms. Kidd, and this house has fallen under a scrutinizing eye. There are dangers ahead that you can scarcely imagine, and I'm here to put this house in order. Tell me, young lady, what do you know of the Incident of 1899?"

Daisy wasn't expecting a history quiz and had to think hard for details. "Let me think. I guess just what everybody in the Society knows," she answered. "In 1899, something happened that removed our connection with the Wonderous Science for a generation, and the Laurel Society had to rebuild from scratch."

"Essentially, yes. Our society has been active for over two centuries, maintaining, nurturing, and protecting the secrets of the magical arts. It is our solemn duty and one that was entrusted to us during a time of great upheaval. But since the Incident, we have struggled to keep our order alive after losing a great deal of accumulated knowledge. The number of people demonstrating the promise of learning the Wonderous Science has been far lower than any time in history. The Watchers division uses our power to locate those that have the potential through peering into their possible futures. For most people, their potential paths through life diminish with age, becoming narrower and narrower with the passage of time. Those with creativity and spirit maintain more of their potential paths, but those that have the potential to be practitioners of the Wonderous Science almost glow with possibility. This is how we determine who your young charges will be. For over one hundred years we have recruited those we could, and nurtured the talent in those that could even touch on a fraction of it, and because of that some of the greatest minds of the past few generations have been inspired by us."

"Yeah. Didn't that billionaire computer genius have a Warden as a nanny?" Daisy said.

"Yes, and a few of his collaborators."

"What about that musician? You know, the one with the glove..."

"Yes, but we try not to talk about that one."

"And what about..."

"Yes, yes, a great many artists, engineers, scientists, and leaders have been guided by the Society, from Nikola Tesla to Louie Armstrong."

"Louie who?"

Mr. Flint closed his eyes in frustration. "The point I'm trying to make, Ms. Kidd, is that the Warden's responsibilities have become more important with every passing year. We need to protect the proud tradition of this institution, and the future of the Wonderous Science in this world. To that end, the New York office has sent me here to tighten things up."

Daisy stopped smiling and swallowed hard. "Tighten things up?" she said. "I'm not sure I understand what you mean."

Mr. Flint stood and crossed his arms behind his back, staring pensively out the window. "I've been tasked with getting the chapter house up to par," he said stiffly. "Things here have been run a little haphazardly for some time, and that is no longer acceptable. We have had… problems with other offices in recent months; everything from theft of artifacts, missing wonderous instruments, and even disappearances. We can't allow that kind of thing to happen here."

"Really?" Daisy sat forward on the edge of her seat. "I hadn't heard. Has there been an investigation? Do you think something like that could happen in Portland?"

Flint turned and looked blankly at her. "The details of the situation really aren't your concern. What is your concern, however, is your future with the Laurel Society." He opened a drawer, pulled out a red folder and laid it ominously on the table. A picture of Daisy was clipped on the corner. "This is your field report. You'll find notes there, records, and detailed complaints about your work in the Wardens division, which is surprising since you have only been there for less than a year. Two of these, including today's fiasco, required intervention by the Stewards – one of them involving a talking bear?"

"A giant talking teddy bear!" she replied, almost laughing. "I thought it was so funny. The kids enjoyed it, but then it got into the kitchen and started eating out of the fridge and their parents thought it was going to maul someone. They didn't get the humor of the whole thing."

Mr. Flint did not look amused. "You do realize that the incident required Level 3 containment, memory wipes, repairs to the client's home, and the waste of valuable society resources?"

"Yeah." Daisy felt her heart sink to her shoes. "I guess I've gotten off to a rocky start," she murmured.

"That is an understatement. Unfortunately, we can no longer afford our operatives operating at a subpar level," he sat down again, this time holding his hands with his fingers interlocked, and looked over the rim of his spectacles. "You are dangerously close to losing your position, Ms. Kidd. We can't let someone with your talent go, but you may be returned to the Stewards department permanently. I know that up until now you have been afforded a certain amount of leniency since your aunt is the Mildred Mizner, but that kind of nepotism can't be tolerated in this current climate."

"Nepotism?" Daisy said, and raised her eyebrow.

"Yes, Ms. Kidd. Favoritism because of your family ties."

"Oh, not Aunt Mizzy!" she said, half offended and half pleading. "She doesn't favor anyone unless they earn it. She said that I could only be a Warden if I worked hard at it, and I've worked so hard! She'd be so disappointed if I got booted out."

"Be that as it may, something must be done, so…" he paused, considering his next words. "I am going to give you one more chance to stay on with the Wardens."

"OH THANK YOU MR. FLINT!" Daisy blurted out. She wanted to hug him, but Flint held up his hand.

"Don't thank me yet. This is could be a…delicate case, and one I would rather give to a proven field operative, but there are some here who still have confidence in your abilities. However, the New York Office requested a junior Warden for this assignment." Once again Mr. Flint reached into his drawer, this time removing a curious looking implement: a round translucent glass, about the size of a dinner plate, set in a copper ring and mounted on a spinning pedestal. He sat it down between them, removed his spectacles, and sat them in a small groove in the base. There was a series of whirrs and clicks, and the glass began to spin and emanate a golden glow.

"Wow! Aunt Mizzy had to draw out all her visions."

"It's a chronal-vision projector – far more accurate than simple sketches," Mr. Flint said. Suddenly, the image of a young girl appeared within the glow. "Meet one of your new charges. Her name is Zora Sparks, and you are going to be her new nanny."

The girl was about twelve with bright hazel eyes, red-brown skin with a slight dusting of almost invisible freckles, and thick textured hair that seem to shoot straight up from her head. She was very pretty, but there was something about the set of her mouth and her eyes that made Daisy feel like she was looking at a stern school teacher.

"Isn't she a little old for a nanny?"

"Not at all. Besides, she has a younger brother who will be your charge as well."

"Great! Sister and brother. I'm so excited! When do I start?"

"Don't get ahead of yourself, Ms. Kidd." Flint removed his spectacles from the apparatus and the image quickly faded. "The boy has displayed some curious abilities, but he is of little interest to me. The girl is the priority, and may have potential that could be of use to the Society. I have seen her in a vision, but the details are fuzzy at best. All I've been able to determine is that she has a high level of natural skill in the Wonderous Science – possibly even Adept level abilities. Then again, she could possibly be of no importance at all."

Daisy's breath caught in her throat. "An Adept? We haven't found an Adept in Portland in years."

"Which is why this is a delicate situation. Adepts are self-taught in the Wonderous Science, go undetected for years, and have a tendency towards being unpredictable. They dabble in elements of wild magic, and tend to be untrusting of people asking about their abilities. This is known to develop into… disturbing behaviors that make them dangerous. You can understand my apprehension in passing this along to you?"

"Yes, Sir."

"Good." Mr. Flint stood and walked to the door, and motioned Daisy to follow. When he opened it, he handed Daisy a small, black folder with the Society crest emblazoned on the cover. The tab on its edge read Subject #215. "Here is what we were able to pull together. It's not much, but gathering the rest of her information is up to you. Your job will be to observe her, determine if she has been using her abilities, and report back to me. Inside you'll find the address and your supply list. Tomorrow you'll meet with their foster mother, a Ms.

Teresa Madison. Stop by the workshop before you leave to be outfitted."

Daisy clutched the folder to her chest, beaming, and turned to leave, but before she could cross the threshold Mr. Flint stopped her short.

"Remember Ms. Kidd, although this is just a child, you must remain vigilant. The Laurel Society has performed our mission for centuries, and in that time we've made our fair share of enemies. Always be watchful."

"Enemies, sir?" Daisy said, her smile fading just a bit. "But this is Portland – what kind of enemies should I be watchful for?"

Mr. Flint looked down at her, his expression grave. "The kind you would least expect," he said, his voice seeming to echo between them, cold and distant for a moment, but quickly returning to its previous tone. "Goodbye, Ms. Kidd. I hope to hear positive reports."

"Yes, sir. Thank you, sir," Daisy said, and shook his hand (maybe a little too hard.) "I promise you won't regret this. I won't let you down."

"See that you don't, Ms. Kidd."

The door closed loudly as she left, and Daisy was reminded of the folded paper in her pocket that Aunt Mizzy had given her. When she opened it, there was a drawing in her aunt's calligraphic style. Staring back at her was the girl from Mr. Flint's vision – the girl whose folder she now held. Zora Sparks. Next to the drawing were words, quickly written.

THE GIRL IS VERY IMPORTANT.
TELL NO ONE.

MR. FLINT
THE WATCHER

TINKERS AND TAILORS

Stephanie met Daisy at the base of the stairs with a consoling smile – a look Daisy had grown all too familiar with.

"I'm so sorry, sweety. I know it couldn't have been good news," she said, taking Daisy's hands and patting them as if she had just heard she had lost a puppy.

Daisy straightened her back and held her chin out proudly. "For your information, it was great news," she said with a big grin. "I've got a new assignment!"

"What?"

"I know, right? Mr. Flint did say I need to do better, but he gave me another chance to make things right – it's a nanny position here in town."

Stephanie looked a little surprised. "That is great news. Congratulations," she said and smiled graciously.

"Thanks. I start tomorrow."

"Well, let's not waste any time then."

Together they walked down the steps to the bottom floor of the house. They came to a narrow hallway with brick red carpet and plain beige walls, at the end of which stood a dark wooden door with a bronze symbol of a hammer crossed with a threaded needle set in its center. The air around it smelled slightly of ozone, coppery and electric.

"I haven't been to this part of the house in ages," Daisy said. "I use to bring messages from Mr. Porter down and drop them in the mail chute for the Tinkers, but he told me to never touch the door."

"It wouldn't have done anything," Stephanie said, "we haven't had a Tinker or Tailor in this part of the country in over forty years. Our new guests came with Mr. Flint's group.

"So you're sure this is ok?" Daisy asked. "I thought junior Wardens weren't allowed to go to the workshop."

"You're with me, dear, and I'm making an exception for you just this once," Steph replied with an uncharacteristic wink. They stood together, hands at their sides, and Stephanie reached up and tapped three times on the symbol with her laurel ring. The sound reverberated in the close hallway like a high-pitched bell. All at once the surface of the door rippled like a disturbed pool, then swirled into a twisting tunnel of stars, quickly receding back like water in a horizontal drain, pulling both women into it. For a moment, Daisy felt like she was floating weightless in space, surrounded by tiny pinpricks of blue light that filled her field of vision. It felt like she had screamed a little, but the space was soundless and serene. Before she could truly react, she felt her body land roughly on solid ground, and the starry expanse immediately disappeared. Now she was laying in front of the door once again but in a different hallway with a floor of cold, flat stone, same as the walls.

"What just happened?" she said breathlessly as she slowly stood. Stephanie didn't attempt to help her up.

"Short-distance spatial shift," Steph replied, matter-of-fact. "The Society lab is off-site, and they keep its location secret. The door in the chapter house is just a shift point."

"So where are we now?" Just as she spoke, the door slowly opened and a mop of curly brown hair poked out.

"Hiya Daisy!"

"Oh my gosh! Johann!" Daisy threw her arms around the familiar thin face that came through the doorway.

"Yeah, it's me alright," came a muffled and slightly choked voice. "It's good to see you."

Noticing a look of disapproval flash across Stephanie's face, Daisy realized she was strangling her oldest friend in the world and quickly released him, trying her best to regain some semblance of composure. "It's been a while," she said nonchalantly. "Two years, right – since you start your training? I thought you were headed for Chicago."

Johann nervously ran his fingers through his hair and tugged at his pinstriped vest. "I was there for a while but came back about a month ago. Guess I was a little homesick. Who needs the Windy City when you've got Stumptown, right? Besides, there have been some recent discoveries here that I just couldn't pass up…"

"Ahem." Stephanie cleared her throat pointedly. "Good to see you know each other. Can we continue this reunion inside?"

"Of course! Come in. Please forgive the mess." Johann blushed, and eagerly welcomed them through the doorway.

The inside of the Tinkers and Tailors workshop was something out of a steam-powered dream. The room was large, and filled with tall shelves on each wall filled with bizarre, amazing machines and implements. The air carried the scent of instrument oil and metal polish, with a slight hint of stale coffee. The sound of gears shifting and clink of small mechanisms whirling filled the space with a soft ambiance. Wide, rectangular tables were arrayed evenly down the middle of the room in rows of two under the hanging lamps – their tops covered with brass, steel, and sometimes stone components that glowed in the dim light. At the tables, five men sat in deep focus, all wearing dark waistcoats and pinstriped slacks, and all hard at work fabricating and repairing different wonderous items and periodically exchanging brief words with one another. Daisy recognized one of them from a meeting she had attended and remembered his name was Mr. Turpin, but the other four were strangers.

"Is it always this busy?" she whispered to Johann. "I didn't know Portland had this kind of staff on hand."

"No. Usually, it's dull as a tomb in here – just me and Greg Turpin over there, and he doesn't talk much – but with everything that is going on, Mr. Flint brought along his own group from New York. They even brought a Tailor with them. Junior level, but still impressive. All of this is to help with working on the artifacts..."

"Not giving away all of our secrets, are you, Joe?" One of the men at the tables had stood up, and was now walking towards them just as Johann had closed the lab door behind Daisy.

"What? Not me! These are Wardens from the main office coming in for outfitting. Ms. Kidd and Ms. Love, this is Marco Faulk. He's the new Tailor I was telling you about."

Having a Tailor in Portland was an odd privilege, to say the least. There were so few of them now that they were usually stationed in larger cities. Their ability to weave magic into material and fabrics made them very important to the Society. They could craft uniforms with built in effects like spatial voids, temperature controls, self-repair, and shielding. Daisy had always imagined them as old men with wispy hair and wrinkled arthritic hands. Marco, of course, looked nothing like that. He had to be in his early twenties, six feet tall, slender, but with wide shoulders like an Olympic swimmer. His chestnut hair was neatly trimmed except for one lock that fell casually over his eyes.

"Nice to meet you," he said, extending his hand. He greeted them with a slight nod and a crooked smile, and Daisy felt herself blush a little when he spoke. "Joe's right of course, I am the new guy – around here anyways, but I've been doing this for long enough that I can be of assistance."

"We don't mind your help! I always need help," Daisy blurted out, instantly realizing how awkward it sounded.

"Thank you, Mr. Faulk. I'm sure you are capable enough to assist with our equipment. Daisy, please stay here and wait for me. Junior Wardens are not allowed in

the WI vault. We don't want you setting anything off."
Stephanie followed Marco out of the room, leaving her
with Johann and the other Tinkers.

"Nice lady," Johann whispered.

"You get used to her, after a while," Daisy replied,
"She's been really patient with me. Believe it or not, I'm
not that great at this stuff."

"I have a hard time imagining that. You were always
so talented."

"Sure, with wild magic – the kind of stuff that isn't
supposed to do anything specific. Now I have all these
crazy tools just making everything more complicated!"
Daisy stopped and noticed the curious look on Johann's
face and suddenly felt a little silly. "Never mind, I
shouldn't be complaining."

"Oh no, continue," Johann smiled. " I totally understand what you mean. Sometimes all these instruments
get in the way of doing something truly magical."

"But you're a Tinker. You work on wonderous items.
Aren't you supposed to, I don't know, love this stuff?"

Johann looked over his shoulder, checking to see if
the men at the tables were paying them any attention.
"Give me your hat and come with me," he said under
his breath, then turned to the other men at the tables
and said, "Ms. Kidd has some problems with her bowler.
I'm taking her to the back to make repairs," to which

they nodded absently. Johann led her to his work area in the far corner, separated from the rest of room by the divider wall. Daisy couldn't help but laugh quietly to herself when she saw his space covered with half completed projects. Johann had always been brilliant, but just a little bit absent-minded. As soon as one idea was in the works, another would come and fight for space in his enormous brain. When they were kids, he and Daisy had started work on a treehouse one spring day after school. Johann had the amazing idea to put a working telescope in the roof so they could look up at the stars on clear nights, so he left Daisy to finish just about everything else. Two days and many splinters later, she had found him in his room turning their telescope into a giant laser. The tree house never did get a roof.

So now, she was surprised to see him place something that appeared to be finished on the table. Inside of small, velvet lined box was a pocket watch, about the size of an open palm, made of polished brass with a silver chain and a laurel motif engraved on its face.

"Wow, Joe. It's beautiful. Did you make this?"

"Most of it, yeah. I found some of the parts in with the artifacts Mr. Flint brought. Mostly it's small components that were probably going to be discarded anyway."

"Artifacts? What exactly are you talking about?" That was the second time that he had mentioned artifacts since she had arrived, which was beginning to tease her curiosity. She couldn't help but notice the question made him a little nervous.

"Never mind that part. What I wanted to show you was this." Johann clicked open the lid and handed it to Daisy. The intricately inlaid face was beautiful, but not that of a regular clock. Instead, it looked more like some kind of stopwatch, with hash marks for up to thirty minutes. She could see the elaborate organization of gears inside, motionless at the moment, but on closer examination, Daisy noticed something strange. The gears seemed to flash blue when they caught the light, each one covered with an elaborate array of arcane symbols.

"Johann, is this a W.I.?" she said, eyes bulging. "You made a W.I.?"

"Quiet. Don't let the others hear you," Johann whispered, the corners of his mouth starting to turn up into a mischievous grin.

The whole thing was ridiculous, of course. No one had made a wonderous item in at least one hundred and fifty years – many thought that it wasn't even possible anymore. It was a lost skill. These magical instruments were created by combining separate parts, each meticulous crafted and imbued with powers to affect the laws of nature. Each part would then work in combination with the others to shift and bend the very fabric of reality. The best a modern day Tinker could do was mend a W.I. the Society already possessed, each one collected and preserved through the centuries. Even a master Tinker could only ever hope to improve or copy one, never actually craft one from scratch.

"How did you do this?" Daisy whispered.

"I was just fooling around with some spare parts, and presto." He smiled, adjusting his glasses on his nose. "Truth be told, I'm not sure if it even works. The curse of the Tinker, I'm afraid. We can work with W.I.s, but we don't have the talent to use them to their full extent." Suddenly Johann's eyes took on a distant sort of sparkle. "That is, of course, what we have you guys for."

"What's that look? I'm not sure I like that look." Daisy said, backing away slowly.

"Come on, Dee! Just try it out for me," he said with a sheepish grin. "It works on very clear principles. The Wonderous Science, as you know, is meant to bring the elements of wild magic under control. People like you, whose talents lie in less regimented forms of magic sometimes have a hard time with W.I.s because of those restrictions. This will help. I promise it's perfectly safe."

"You used to say that a lot when we were kids. Remember that curling iron you 'fixed' for me? Perfectly safe, you said."

"Yeah. I don't know what you are still sore about – all of your hair grew back eventually. This is different. I guarantee you won't regret it."

Daisy stared hard at her grinning friend and felt her resolve melt away like a butterscotch on her tongue. Johann had a way of smiling at her that let her guard down. "Fine," she said, "Give it to me. If this thing blows up, I'll never forgive you."

"Marvelous! Now take it in your right hand. I'll set the timer to ten seconds."

The watch was light and gave her hand a slight tingle as she touched it. "Now what?" she said.

"Hold an image in your mind of what you want it to do, then click the top. Simple right?" Johann replied, and backed away two steps. "It'll be fine."

Fine, he says. Daisy drew in a full breath and pressed down on the button at the top of the watch. Instantly, she felt a rush of sensation, like touching her tongue against a battery – only with her whole body. There was a soft sound, like machinery starting up, and before she could react all of the items on Johann's work bench began to shimmer with warm light, folding and twisting into strange amorphous shapes, then floating quickly up from their places and spreading wings of molten gold. Each one swooped around her head for a split second to the soft sound of metallic music, then landed on her and Johann's shoulders.

"What's going on back there?" a voice said from the lab, but before the speaker could approach, the objects returned to their original shapes and fell clattering to the floor.

"NOTHING! Nothing special. Just working!" Johann croaked just as Stephanie appeared around the corner with Marco Faulk, who was holding a large box filled with brass instruments covered in gyros, gears, and dials.

"Wow, Joe. Your space is filthier than yesterday. I didn't think it was possible." said Marco, noticing the floor covered with bits and pieces. "You might want to get a broom."

"I was just telling him that," Daisy giggled, wiping her sweaty palms together. She noticed Johann had stopped breathing, but tried to act natural. "You ready to go, Steph?"

Stephanie reached up and removed Daisy's bowler and turned it upside down. Taking the box from Marco, she emptied the entire contents into the hat. As the last of tools disappeared into the hat's bottomless expanse, she returned it to Daisy and said, "Now we're ready. Say your goodbyes and I'll meet you at the door."

As she and Marco moved out of earshot, Johann finally took in a nervous breath and crumbled onto his stool.

"That was so close! I think I almost had a heart attack. I'm surprised they couldn't hear it pounding through my chest," he said, running his fingers nervously through his hair. "But that was incredible! It works way better than I had anticipated."

"Seriously?" said Daisy, flabbergasted. "What just happened? It was like ten different things happened at once!"

"Pretty accurate assessment. First off, what were you thinking?"

"Butterflies," she replied. "Orange ones."

"Hmm, those shapes weren't exactly butterflies, but they were pretty close. That's what it does, you see. That device causes innumerable wonderous events to happen simultaneously – all you have to do is guide them with your mind. Once it's ready, you won't need to have all of the items you're carrying in your hat. Just this. I call it the Splendid Machine. Cool, huh?"

Daisy couldn't take her eyes off of it, her mind filled with images of success and praise. This could solve all of my problems, she thought to herself. "Johann," she said, "any chance you would let me borrow it? Just for a little while?"

"What? Are you crazy?" Johann took the watch from her open hand and placed it back into the box it came from "Daisy, it's barely been tested. We only had it set for ten seconds, and you saw what it made. It needs more work before I'm ready to let anyone know about it."

"Please, Joe. This could change everything. I promise I'll be careful…"

"Out of the question! I don't want you to get hurt."

From the other room, Marco called out. "Come on, Joe! Time's a wastin'. I need your notes on the first cycle of tests from this morning."

"Coming!" Johann scrambled for his papers, which lay scattered about the floor. With Daisy's help, he gathered them up into an unwieldy pile. "Thanks, Dee," he said, straightening his vest and glasses. "Look, I'm sorry that I can't be of more help."

"Don't worry about it," she replied, jabbing his shoulder. "Go on. I'll see you around, ok?"

"Ok."

As he left, Daisy turned her attention to the watch, sitting quietly in the box on the table. She hesitated for a split second, then hastily grabbed a scrap of paper and scribbled a quick note.

Sorry, Joe. I promise to bring it back soon. Your Friend, Dee.

She sat the note in the box, closed it, and placed the Splendid Machine in her pocket.

"He'll understand," said Daisy to her own conscience, and ran to meet Stephanie at the door.

STEPHANIE LOVE
THE PARAGON

ZORA SPARKS

ust breathe, Daisy thought cheerily. *It's only your whole future on the line.*

She had arrived at the large craftsman style house at 1515 Anders Place and now stood inches from the front gate, summoning up her courage. Against Stephanie's suggestions, she had taken a cab instead of flying – no use adding another gut-wrenching element to the day.

The house sat in a nice neighborhood, surrounded by manicured yards and well-tended gardens on either side. She couldn't help but notice that this house, in particular, had more "special amenities" than the others. There were wind turbines on the roof, a solar-powered automatic gate, and what appeared to be small mechanical birds perched on the railing of the porch... watching her with clicking robotic eyes. There was also a disturbing number of blast holes in the lawn, but Daisy chose to ignore that and focus on the task at hand. She pulled out the notes Mr. Flint had given her along with her orders and looked them over one more time. "What's the worst that could happen?" she said, "Basically it's just a 12-year-old girl who may or may not have super powers and her eight-year-old brother…with a red level disciplinary record?" That was usually reserved for… troubled kids. She looked again to make sure she had read that correctly. "Great. What have I gotten myself into?"

When she got to the door, Daisy quickly straightened her skirt and her coat. She checked her hat as well, in which she had placed a single daisy in the ribbon for luck. Her experiences with children had not gone well on previous assignments, so she needed all the luck she could get. Just as she raised her hand to knock, she heard a peculiar sound. Looking down, she noticed a small peep hole which opened with a mechanical whirl.

"State your business!" a deep, distorted voice said from out of nowhere, sounding like a bad movie villain.

There was an awkward pause before Daisy replied. "Hello? My name is Daisy Kidd. Is this the Madison residence?"

"That didn't answer my question. What is your business?" the voice said. The peephole shot up to

Daisy's height along a hidden track set into the door, and a small scope extended, focusing sharply on her face. The eyepiece opened wide like the shutter of a camera, and Daisy could see her confused reflection on the lens within.

"I'm the new nanny from the agency, and I have an appointment."

"Nobody told me," said the voice, almost mockingly. "You got any identification?"

"No. I'm a nanny – I don't have a badge or anything!"

"Well, you got some paperwork or something, lady? I'm not opening up for just anybody."

Daisy could feel her face getting flush like it always did when she was annoyed. She lifted up the folder Mr. Flint had given her and held it close to the peep hole. "See, I have a file with Ms. Teresa Madison's name on it, as well as Zora and Nathaniel Sparks. I'm from the agency. Are you going to let me in or not?" she said, arms crossed. "I know you can't be Ms. Madison, so whoever you are, you had better start taking me seriously."

She heard the latch unlock, and the door opened just enough to reveal a boy. He was short and stocky with dark skin and a close haircut. He wore a leather vest and large mirror shades and stood in the threshold like some kind of bodyguard.

"The nanny, huh," he said, his face straight and direct. "That's a weird hat you're wearing. You sure you aren't a chimney sweep?"

"Those are weird shades you're wearing. Sure you aren't a motorcycle cop?" she replied, but regretted getting snarky right off the bat. Great start, Daisy, she thought to herself. Oddly enough, the little boy cracked a smile and removed the shades.

"You seem ok," he grinned and opened the door. "Come on in, and I'll go get Teresa. She told me to open up if it was you."

"So what's with the third degree?"

"Can't be too careful," he said and waved her inside.

The boy showed Daisy to the living room. It was nicely decorated, though maybe a little boring for Daisy's tastes, and at the moment smelled like something was burning.

"Take a seat," said a voice from the kitchen. "I'll be out in a second. Having a little bit of a problem with the stove."

Daisy sat down, and seconds later in walked a small woman with dark rimmed glasses. She was a little older than Daisy and had a welcoming smile, though slightly frazzled at the moment, warm auburn skin, and dark, curly hair that was a little singed on the ends. She had patches of flour on her face, and she wore a floral apron covered in cooking stains. Daisy then noticed she was carrying what could only have been described as a plate of charcoal briquettes.

"Ms. Kidd! I'm so glad you could make it," she said and nervously shook Daisy's hand (it was sticky with bits of dough.) "Would you like a cookie? This is my first batch, so they didn't turn out the way I was expecting. I've never been that great at baking. Zora helped me fix the stove the other day, but I think she gave it a little more UMPH than necessary." Daisy heard the oven roar a bit beyond the kitchen doorway like a freshly stoked blast furnace.

"Sure, thanks. And you can call me Daisy if you like." Daisy took a cookie from the tray. "I hope this isn't a bad time?"

"NO! Never. I'm just glad you're even here. After what happened with the last nanny, I was afraid that the agency wasn't going to send anyone else and just cut us off completely," she laughed grimly.

Daisy stopped short of putting the cookie in her mouth. "What happened with the last nanny?"

Teresa blushed and sat down. "Oh, nothing really. We just had a little incident with some dye. Honestly, I'm not even quite sure how it got in the house. I won't bore you with the details, but let's just say it was non-toxic and I've been assured that her skin will turn back to its normal color in a few more weeks."

"Personally, I thought she looked good in blue," the boy said with a smile. Teresa wasn't as amused.

"I think everybody can add a little color to their wardrobe every now and again," said Daisy, interjecting into the tense moment. "Why not blue skin!"

Nate beamed. "That's exactly what I said."

"Do me a favor, smarty pants, and go get your sister," said Teresa. As the boy left, he looked down at the cookie in Daisy's hand and shook his head.

"Don't eat that," he whispered. "She means well, but trust me you'll be glad you didn't," then darted up the stairs.

"That's Nate, by the way," Teresa said after he was out of earshot. "He's a bit of a handful, but basically a sweet kid. In fact, he reminds me of his mother – he acts tough, but under all that he's just a marshmallow."

"Oh, I was told they were your foster children." Daisy took a quick glance at her notes to make sure. "I didn't know you were in contact with their biological parents."

"I'm not – not anymore," Teresa said with a sad smile. "Zora and Nate are my sister's children – Jennifer Sparks. She's...in the hospital, and the kids don't know their dad, so they're here with me."

Daisy put the folder away. "I'm so sorry," she said and meant it. "I didn't mean to bring up anything painful."

"Oh, that's alright. Jenny and I hadn't really spoken in years. Our parents passed when I was just a baby, and since we didn't have any other family, we were put in foster care. We were in different homes, and I was eventually adopted, but Jenny moved around a lot. Even when she got on her own she was always traveling, but I would get a letter from her from time to time. Then a few months ago, I get a call from social services that I have a niece and nephew in need of a home."

"Wow! Lucky they had you," said Daisy reassuringly. "I'm sure their mom is glad they're with you."

Teresa looked unsure how to reply to the compliment. "I guess lucky is the word. Honestly, it all worked out in a pretty strange way. I just moved back into this house. Our parent's left it to both me and Jenny in their will I guess, and I really never had any plan on living in it, but when foster care told me about Nate and Zora, I figured why not! Zora actually set most of it up. So here we are, and we've been alright for the most part, but…" she paused, looking a little embarrassed, then continued in a hushed voice. "I'm not that great with kids. The truth is I've never lived with anybody, especially children. I work for a hotel. I'm sure you've heard of Sleep Right Inns?"

Daisy shook her head. "Sorry, not really," she replied.

Teresa looked disappointed, but picked the conversation right back up, "Oh well, that's ok. A lot of people haven't. We're getting bigger, though. I'm a regional manager, and the job – primarily my boss – is super demanding. Add on top of that the kid's 'special needs'…"

More surprises. "What 'special needs' exactly? Does this have to do with…Nathaniel's school disciplinary record?" Daisy asked.

"Oh, that. That was blown way out of proportion. Just a couple of little fights at school," Teresa said. "Nate is always trying to protect his sister, even though she's older. A month ago at the bus stop, some kid says something mean and boom! It shouldn't have blown up into such a thing – but I guess it didn't help that Nate could be registered as a deadly weapon."

Daisy's eyes got big when she heard this. "Excuse me? That's not in my file."

"Surprise," Teresa mumbled. "He's a black belt in four different martial arts – five once he's done with Aikido. He started last week."

"That's fast!"

"That's nothing. He's a muscle-mimic, so he can learn most physical stuff just by watching. I wish he'd try the violin or something, but all he want's to do is watch kung-fu movies and cartoons. But don't worry, he wouldn't hurt a fly, and is usually harmless unless it has something to do with Zora. She's the real issue."

Here we go. "I was told by the agency that she's pretty smart. Gifted even."

Teresa look around the room quickly to see if the children were coming down, then leaned in close to Daisy. "Smart? Is that all they told you?" She stifled a tired laugh. "The girl is a genius. No other word for it. She has an IQ of 172, has basically already graduated from high school, and can make or repair anything you could think of. Computers, machinery – heck, she changed the transmission out on my car last week."

Behind the admiration in her eyes, Daisy thought she saw something else – something bordering on fear. "With a girl that smart, it's not hard to see why she doesn't think she needs anyone telling her what to do," Teresa said, resting her chin on her fists. "She's willful and opinionated, and basically thinks that I'm useless, which is how most twelve-year-old girls are I guess. The problem is that most twelve-year-old girls aren't building jetpacks in their room."

Daisy took the rather useless folder Mr. Flint had given her and set it on the chair beside her. "Wow. There is a lot they didn't tell me," she said, feeling a little overwhelmed. The girl was a possible Adept, which was amazing enough, but add onto that genius and martial arts master little brother and Daisy could feel her head starting to spin.

"It's a bit much, I know. That's why we've been through so many nannies and sitters," Teresa said. "I'll understand if you think it's not the position for you."

In that instant, something clicked in Daisy's head. "Don't worry, Ms. Madison!" she blurted out. "I'm the woman for the job!"

Teresa jumped forward and wrapped her arms around Daisy's neck, laughing hysterically. "Thank you! Thank you! Thank you!" she said, "And please, call me Teresa. I promise you won't regret it. They're just going to love you, Daisy, I know…" Just then, they both noticed the burnt smell had gotten stronger, and whiffs of black smoke were floating in from the kitchen doorway. "THE COOKIES! I TOTALLY FORGOT!" and she bolted out of the room.

<hr />

While Teresa handled her second batch of chocolate chip cinders, Daisy took the moment to examine the house. Reaching into her hat, she produced a thin, silver cylinder about the length of an ink pen. She pressed the copper button on the side, and the tip of the cylinder swirled opened like a flower unfolding its petals. A blue light issued forth, and Daisy moved it through the air in a wide arch, closed it, and looked at the small gauge on the bottom, which read:

35% etherea residue detected.

"That's strange," Daisy thought. Usually, when someone used the Wonderous Science, they raised the level of magic energy around them, especially around those that didn't know how to use their powers. These levels were only slightly over normal – not high enough for a true practitioner.

"What exactly are you doing?" said a calm voice from behind Daisy which sent her jumping for the ceiling. When she turned, standing before her was the girl from the drawing, and from Mr. Flint's chronal-vision projector – the same intelligent brown eyes, wild hair, and stern set to her mouth. She wore a high collared frock coat, purple, that hung down to tops of her high black boots, and perched on the top of her head was a peculiar set of goggles. She held her hands behind her thin frame, like a captain waiting for a report from some lowly private.

"Oh nothing much," Daisy replied, slipping the tool into her pocket. "Just checking for…mold spores. I'm sort of allergic." She extended her hand. "You must be Zora. My name is Ms. Daisy Kidd, but you can call me Daisy. I'll be your new nanny."

"Is that so," the girl replied. She looked her up and down as if she were examining each and every visible detail. "You're younger than the others, with a hint of 'amateur' about you."

Daisy's face went red. "I've been at this longer than you think," she said.

"Let me be the judge of that." Zora pulled down her goggles and took Daisy's hand, extending one eyepiece. There was a quick flash of light, followed by a slight humming sound. "You have cake residue on your skin. Pink frosting. Minimal wear to your hands says that you haven't worked much, and based on your accent and clothing I figure you've never left Portland in your life, which denotes a lack of initiative." She lifted the goggles back up to the top of her head. "All and all, I'm guessing underachiever, am I right? But there is something else. Something…unexpected."

Daisy snatched her hand back. "Wow, I guess you've got me all figured out then," she grumbled.

"Not really. What I really want to know is why you're sweeping our house for energy signatures?" Zora cocked her head slightly to the side and grinned a knowing sort of grin that never seems to touch her eyes, which were leveled unblinkingly at the strange young woman in front of her. Zora lifted her hand, which Daisy had only just then noticed was covered in an elaborate glove with metallic fingertips, and with a flourish she snapped her fingers like a match striking a flint. The air around her hand glimmered faintly for a moment, like a haze of rainbow light, before fading away. "Personally, I like to check this way. Did you find what you were looking for?" Before Daisy could answer, Nate came bounding down the stairs.

"You being nice, Zoe?" said Nate as he walked slowly up to them, lifting a blackened cookie from the plate Teresa had left.

"I'm always nice, Nathan," Zora replied.

"Riiiight." Nate bit down on the cookie and savored it, little dark pieces clinging to his lips.

"I thought you told me not to eat those?" Daisy asked, trying not to give away her astonishment.

"Leaves more for me. I like em' this way."

Teresa returned to the room and found them standing there in a circle like they were in a Mexican standoff (only one of them was armed with a cookie.) "Well, batch two disintegrated, so we'll have to make due with what we have. I see you've all met now," she said. "Daisy is going to be helping out with you guys and staying in the extra bedroom. I'm sure you'll love it, Daisy – you'll have your own bathroom and everything." Teresa turned to Zora and crossed her arms. "She is to be treated with the utmost respect, do you understand? That means no tricks or traps of any kind."

"Any kind?" said Zora.

"Any kind," Teresa replied.

Zora kept a look of calm contemplation on her face before responding simply, "Agreed."

"Excellent! Well, this was kind of a done deal already, but it's nice to have a consensus. Daisy, can you start tomorrow?"

Everything was going pretty fast, but Daisy decided to go with it. "Sure. Of course. I'll need to get a few things but I can be back in the morning."

"Tomorrow is the last day before the Fall break, so come back in the afternoon instead and we'll take a chance to get to know each other a little bit."

"Sounds good to me." Daisy shook Teresa's hand excitedly, but out of the corner of her eye she couldn't help but notice a slight sneer on Zora's face as she did. Their eyes locked for an uncomfortable moment, Zora's gaze getting more intense with each passing second, while Daisy held her own much to Zora's surprise. Teresa broke the stalemate.

"Come on kids, I think it's time for bed!" she said and shuffled Zora and Nate off towards the stairs. "You guys are going to get along just perfect, right kids?"

That's when Zora cracked a smile that sent chills up Daisy's spine. "Oh yes. Just perfect," she said. The smile never reached her eyes.

"She seems pretty nice," Nate said as they reached the top of stairs. "A lot nicer than Mrs. Bunker, with that giant mole on her mouth – or Mrs. Grisham who always smelled like cough syrup. Eww."

"You're way too trusting, brother," said Zora, and nudged him hard on the shoulder with a wink. "If I were you, I'd keep a close eye on this one. There something… different about Ms. Daisy Kidd."

Zora walked slowly down the hall towards her room, her thoughts troubled. She had known this was coming, but not quite so soon. She wasn't ready. She needed more time.

"You just worry too much. What's the worst that could happen?" Nate was headed for the bathroom when he stopped short of the door. "Is she the one? The one you said was coming to hurt us?"

"I'm not sure, Nate." She glanced back and noticed her brother's eyes. He was scared – something she found strangely unnerving. "I guess you and I just have to find out, and quickly."

"Maybe we should just cancel the plan."

Zora didn't turn around as she walked to her room. "No. The plan is still in play."

JUST EVERYDAY WONDEROUS

Daisy spent that night going over every manual she had in her room, from *Small Miracles: The Use of Magic for Inspiration and Illumination* to *More than a Spoonful of Sugar: Wonderous Strategies for Guidance of Young Practitioners*. The Laurel Society basically had "wowing" children down to a precise science, every scenario carefully laid out for maximum impact. It was their main function, so of course, they didn't leave any element to chance. By the time she had gotten through the fifth book in the stack, Daisy was fast asleep and drooling all over her copy of *Constant Vigilance: A Treatise on Children and Etherea Manipulation*.

Morning came like a splash of cold water, and Daisy woke with a start, mortified to find that she was late for roll call, again. She rushed through her shower, dressing quickly and almost tumbling down the stairs just in time to see the rest of the Wardens, Stewards, and the newly arrived Daggers and Tinker-Tailors filing into the library. She made it through the double doors just as they were closing shut, and hustled to take her place amongst the Warden group, her wet red curls still dripping slightly from her pathetic excuse for a shower. She stood straight, as was expected, with her bowler tucked primly under her arm. A few in the rank and file glanced at her from the corners of their eyes. These gatherings at the Portland office only happened once a month, but Daisy was always late to them. At that moment she could feel their judging stares – Stephanie's in particular.

Truth be told, besides Stephanie Love and some of the Stewards like Mr. Porter and Mr. Hawk, Daisy didn't have many friends at the Chapter House. She tried not to worry about it and to just give her best effort, but on days like today, she could feel the butterflies in her stomach stirred into a frenzy with each withering glance.

They were all facing the large bay windows of the library when Mr. Flint, who had been sitting in a leather armchair enjoying his morning coffee, stood up to address them. He looked as sharp as ever, with his crimson red waistcoat and coal black suit and bowler, and he straightened his glasses before speaking.

"Good morning, practitioners," he said. His speech was clipped and in that indiscernible accent. "I have had the pleasure to meet with you all individually, but I'd like to take this time to introduce myself to you as a group. As you know, my name is Arthur Flint, and I will be your new Watcher for the Portland chapter house of the Laurel Society. The New York chapter house has a vested interest in making this city as prosperous as possible. This area of the country has always had a wealth of those with potential to practice the Wonderous Science, and since the Society came to the United States in the early 1800s, Portland has been a hub of education, discovery, and invention." Flint locked his hands behind his back as he spoke, walking slowly down the lines of gathered practitioners. "The ability to use etherea, or magic as non-practitioners are prone to call it, has become rarer and rarer in the past decades. Finding those who have the talent, managing those of our community that operate outside of the societies, and…containing those that would use these gifts for darker purposes is our mission and our calling. We must endeavor to uphold the high standards laid down for us by our illustrious predecessors." When he came to Daisy's place in line, he paused for a moment. "I have no tolerance for mediocrity," he said, "and I'll expect nothing less than perfection from each and every one of you."

Daisy could feel her face flush red hot, and she found herself holding her breath until Mr. Flint returned to the front of the group.

"These gentlemen and ladies," he said, motioning to the Daggers, "are our new transfers from the New York chapter house. You needn't learn their names." He then pointed to Johann and Marco. "Our Tinker-Tailors, Mr. Marco Faulk and your very own Mr. Johann Epstein will be working on special projects in addition to their regular duties, and in an undisclosed location only accessible through the downstairs travel door. Their work is to be kept confidential, so there will be no questions about their assignment under any circumstances. Understood?"

The group answered, "Yes, Watcher," in unison.

"Good," Flint said, straightening his vest. "Best of luck on your assignments today. I know you won't let me or the Society down. Dismissed." Mr. Flint turned quickly and left, followed by Mr. Hobbs and the Daggers.

They disappeared back upstairs, and Daisy felt a collective sigh of relief from the entire room. As the group broke up, everyone returning to their respective assignments, Stephanie stayed behind along with Marco and Johann.

"He's a real bag of sunshine, isn't he?" Marco said when Daisy walked up, flashing that dazzling smile that made Daisy feel an unexpected compulsion to giggle.

"He's been my boss for a while, so I'm kind of used to his chilly demeanor. You'll get used to it too."

"How long did that take?" Stephanie asked, not looking too concerned.

"Fifteen years, give or take," Marco replied. He had a distant sort of look in his eyes. "I grew up in the New York office, so I've known Mr. Flint since I was a kid, but since I'm more Tailor than Tinker, I'm under his radar for the most part. Wardens' really get most of his special attention, and the rest of us don't have too much to fear."

"Speak for yourself," Johann chimed in, nervously running his hands through his hair. "The guy scares the beans out of me."

"I hope I can get used to him, Marco," Daisy said, "that speech felt like he was talking directly to me. I wanted to cover my eyes until it was over."

"That just means that you have to make a better impression on him," Stephanie said, stroking her blonde hair back behind her ear ever so precisely. "The best way to do that is by doing a perfect job with these new charges of yours. Come straight out of the gate and really knock their socks off."

"I'm not sure how I'm supposed to do that," Daisy said, pulling a handful of handwritten notes out of her pocket. "I spent all night going through the manuals, and I can't think of anything that is going to impress these kids."

"Nonsense," Stephanie said, barely noticing the small pile of scribble instructions in Daisy's hands. "Children are easy to impress."

"You don't understand, Steph. This girl – she's talented. She knew I was taking readings in the house, and when she pointed it out her…"

"It doesn't matter, Daisy!" Stephanie said, this time with impatience in her voice. "They're just children. She may have been aware of some magic, or at least have the slightest understanding of etherea, but she's not a practitioner. The last time any of us had a charge that actually knew anything about the Wonderous Science was, um, never! You have to go into that house today and show them you are the boss – and if you can't, fake it."

Daisy wanted to say something but suddenly found all her explanations and arguments rather weak, withering in under Stephanie's absolute assurance. She stuffed the notes back into her pockets and gave a weak nod of agreement. "You're right, Stephanie, of course. I'll think of something."

"That's my girl," she said, patting Daisy on her shoulder.

Daisy's palms were sweating when she returned to the home of her new charges, and when Teresa welcomed her inside, she tried her best to keep her anxieties in check.

"Thanks for coming," Teresa said, a little flushed. "I'm making dinner. Lasagna!"

Daisy noticed a considerable amount of sauce and flour on her apron. "Need any help?" she asked, not wanting to be too forward.

"Oh no, I've got this. You can head upstairs to get the kids ready to eat," Teresa replied, and ran back towards the kitchen. "They are excited to see you!"

Daisy made her way up to the hallway and left at the landing. There were family photos on the wall of an older couple with two daughters and a few more of Zora and Nathan. One, in particular, caught Daisy's eye. In it was a beautiful woman with long curly hair, and on her lap was a young Zora Sparks, no more than seven, and her brother, barely even two years old. The both were smiling, but even then Zora's smile had something behind it − a maturity that belied her age.

When she got to the children's rooms, which were right beside each other, the doors were open. On first glance, Daisy could tell how different their personalities were just by looking at their surroundings. Zora's room was immaculate, everything in its own place, with very few personal items anywhere. The order was almost unnerving. Nathan, on the other hand, was anything but organized– every wall was covered in movie posters featuring Kung Fu, superheroes, and ninjas, along with an assortment of implements, like a pair of homemade nunchucks and what appeared to be a kendo sword, hung haphazardly from coat hooks. Daisy could barely see the floor through the layer of comics, adventure books, and a smattering of old laundry, and right in the middle of the chaos were Zora and Nathan having a heated conversation.

"You need to stop always trying to control everything!" Nathan said, poking his sister in the shoulder. "Not everybody wants to do everything 'Zora's Way.'"

"You don't have a choice, NATHAN. I'm the oldest and we're doing this because I said so…" Zora's voice trailed off when they saw Daisy standing in the doorway. "Oh. You're early," she said, "we weren't expecting you until six."

"I thought I would get here and spend some time with you," Daisy said, stepping into the room, "maybe even help you tidy things up before dinner."

Zora snorted. "Tidy up? Really. That's a wasted effort in this room. Nathan has so much stuff and ground-in mess here…"

"Hey! There's a system," Nate interjected.

"…that you might as well just give up and accept it for what it is. Believe me."

This is it, Daisy. Here's your chance. Daisy said to herself. Technique 205: Magical Room Clean Up. Always a sure fire way to impress new charges. Fake it till you make it. Daisy removed her coat. "I guess we're just going to have to try something a little different then," she said, holding her head high in her best impression of Stephanie Love. She rolled up her sleeves and walked to the middle of the room with her back to them both, removing her bowler as she did. *205 requires a levitator, a #5 objectanimator, and a TK amplifier and regulator,* Daisy thought, running the calculations twice in her head to make sure she remembered them correctly. She then reached deep into the pocket dimension in her bowler. Her arm disappeared up to her shoulder as she rummaged around for a second, activating all the correct wonderous items in the right sequence. Everything was prepared.

"What exactly are you doing?" Zora asked, peeking around Daisy to get a better view, but Daisy was already done and turned to the children with an excited grin.

"We're going to do a little magic," she said loftily, and instantly the door closed with a bang. Daisy raised her hands like a conductor, and when she moved them items began to rise from the floor, swirling and shifting in the air as if dancing to an unheard melody. "Let's straighten out this mess, shall we?"

"Awesome!" Nathan said, watching as his books began to gather into perfectly organized stacks and place themselves on the bookshelf. "Zora, are you seeing this?" Zora was watching, but when Daisy glanced at her from the corner of her eye, the look on her face was not one of happiness, joy, or wonder. It was anger.

"I should have brought some music," Daisy said as she felt her momentary swell of pride deflate under Zora's piercing glare. The objects in the room wavered, and the nunchucks on the wall fell to the ground.

"I think you're done," Zora said and tugged hard on the corner of Daisy's waistcoat. Daisy felt a surge of power in her hands, and suddenly the gentle rhythm guiding the cleanup turned from classical to hard rock. In seconds, the room turned into a maelstrom of toys, magazines, and clothes, rushing from one corner to the other with Zora, Nate, and Daisy in the eye of the storm.

"Watch out!" Nate said, jumping up to grab this kendo sticks before they hit Daisy and Zora. When his feet left the ground, Nate was caught up in the spinning mass of objects.

"Stop this!" Zora growled.

"I'm trying!" Daisy replied, now frantically trying to deactivate the wonderous items in her hat. "It's not supposed to do this. Something isn't working."

"Oh move over!" Zora reached into her pocket and pulled out a small black bell. She held her hands out with the bell held tight, and with one motion she sent out a sharp ring, cutting through the rush of sound in the room. A moment later, all of the items in the room fell to the ground, including Nate who fell into Daisy 's waiting arms.

"How do you know how to dispel magic?" Daisy whispered as everything went still. Before another word was said, the door slowly creaked open and Teresa poked her head into the room.

"Everything alright? I heard a lot of commotion so I figured I'd check in," she said, smiling awkwardly.

"Just fine," Daisy squeaked, setting Nathan down, "just trying to do a little spruce up in here, right kids?"

Zora had a stern expression, but replied, "Yea, just fine."

"Great! Well, get yourselves ready for dinner. You'll be happy to hear that I didn't burn it this time." As she left, Daisy could hear her mumble, "but I'll be glad when Daisy takes over this part."

After the door closed, Zora, Nate, and Daisy stood in awkward silence. "I guess I should explain what you just saw, I mean what just happened," Daisy said.

"Not really," Zora replied. "We don't need to talk about this at all."

"But, that was amazing, right?" Daisy said.

Zora let out a deep sigh. "You're going to have to practice a little more before you get to 'amazing.' That was just dangerous." She opened the door and turned to her brother. "Come on, Nathan. Let's get downstairs before Daisy here does any more damage."

They walked out, but Nate couldn't help giving Daisy a thumbs up and mouthing the words "that was AWESOME!" as they left the room, leaving their new nanny standing in the midst of the disaster she had just wrought. After everything, the malfunction of the wonderous items, and Zora stopping it, the only thought that went through her head was, *This is going to be way harder than I thought.*

TERESA MADISON
THE AUNT

THE MUSEUM AND
THE IRON SOLDIERS

Daisy arrived at the house early with a small bag of clothes, and a potted plant Aunt Mizzy had given her. After spending the whole night going over her Warden's manual to prepare, she felt pretty confident about the second day with the children. She had even cornered Stephanie before leaving the chapter house earlier that morning, hoping to glean a few more ideas.

"Make sure to keep your non-magical supplies handy; cell phone, keys, that kind of thing. People will expect you to have them, but try not to use them too much. You are a mage, after all. You must seem bigger than life to your charges. Remember what the manual says: always be mysterious, magical, grand and extraordinary – the awe of your charges will aid in their growth," Stephanie said in her usual prim manner. "Our job is to inspire wonder, but part of that is earning their admiration. You must always be right no matter what, never abide backtalk, and above all, never show weakness. That is the only way that you'll gain their respect."

"Got it. One problem – I'm not sure I can pull off 'grand and extraordinary,'" Daisy had said.

"Figure out how to 'pull it off.'" Stephanie cooly replied.

So when Teresa met her at the door, Daisy tried her best to be as grand as she could.

"Wow, you're early!" Teresa said, her makeup half done and her glasses sitting slightly askew on her nose. "We're still getting ready."

"Let me help," said Daisy, and she glided inside. "I'll make breakfast while you finish up."

Before long, Daisy had filled the house with the smell of her white chocolate pancakes, fresh coffee, and stacks of bacon. "Grand" may have been a stretch for her, but when it came to cooking, with or without magic, "extraordinary" was her specialty. Teresa and the children gathered at the kitchen table and dug in. Nate took the king's share of the bacon, while Zora seems to be satisfied with a sliced grapefruit and a tall glass of water.

"That was wonderful," Teresa said, as she grabbed her scarf and coat. "What a great start. Here, I have some money for you and the kids. Where ever you want to go is fine with me. Did you have any ideas?"

Before Daisy could speak, Zora said, "The museum," in a very definite tone. "There is an exhibit there on E.W. Rathmore that I've been wanting to go to."

Daisy smiled and nodded. "Then I guess we're off to the museum."

"Great. Did you need extra for cab fare?"

"No worries. We'll be taking an alternative means of transportation," Daisy replied.

Teresa looked confused, but she waved it off. "Ok, but keep an eye out for Nate if you take the train. He has a tendency to wander. Call me on my cell if you run into any problems."

"Oh no, the cell phone." Daisy cringed. She'd totally forgot! "I don't have one yet, but I'm sure we'll be alright today, but I'll make sure to get one for next time."

Teresa looked a little concerned but waved it off with a smile. "I guess that'll have to do." She kissed Nate on the forehead and squeezed Zora's hand gently. "PLEASE, be good you two." With that, she was out the door.

Zora and Nate turned their attention to Daisy. "Alternative transportation, huh," Zora said. "What exactly do you mean by 'alternative?'"

Daisy thought for a second about her response before answering. "Let's put it this way kids. Today you

are going to see some things that you might consider…
amazing."

"Amazing?" Nate said, grinning.

"Yes. Some might call them…extraordinary. Even
impossible."

"Impossible is relative," Zora said, sounding uncon-
vinced. "Can you be more specific?"

"Well, you'll just have to wait and see," Daisy said,
adjusting her bowler hat. At that moment, she was
acutely aware of the weight of Johann's pocket watch in
her coat pocket – almost vibrating with pure possibility.
"Get your things – we're leaving now."

Outside, Daisy stood on the walkway waiting as
the kids came out the front door. Nate was wearing his
mirrored shades again and a light blue jacket, while Zora
was in her long purple coat with a leather satchel slung
over her shoulder.

"I'm ready for some amazing!" Nate said, bouncing
up to her, while Zora approached with a look of concern.

"Good. Now both of you take each other's hand."

They did as she asked – Zora grudgingly, though.
Then, Daisy removed her hat and adjusted the
Anti-gravitator band inside, making sure to press the
button for the cloaking shield. She pulled it down tight

on her head so that it almost covered her eyes and ears, then took a long shaky breath.

"I'm not sure what's going on here, but why do I get a distinct feeling that you don't know what you're doing?" Zora said.

Daisy couldn't help but laugh nervously. "I guess you'll just have to trust me," she said with a slightly aloof tenor to her voice, thinking all the while "Be extraordinary." Squaring her shoulders, she took the children's hands, bent her knees, and kicked off from the ground.

Instantly she felt that strange feeling in her stomach, like sitting in a roller coaster car at the peak of a drop. She looked down and watched as their feet lifted from the stone walkway, their bodies surrounded by a shimmering glow. Nate and Zora's stunned silence filled Daisy with a giddy sense of accomplishment. "Now hold on tight kids!" Then, they were off – flying over their house and up past the tops of the autumn colored trees. Daisy felt Zora's grip tighten, and looked back and saw her eyes big with stifled surprise. Daisy wasn't sure what to expect. One could anticipate two kids to do any number of things in this situation: scream in terror, claw at your arm, pass out, or in the best case scenario, squeal in delight. Zora seemed to be just trying her best to stay calm – Nate, on the other hand, was going a different route.

"ALRIGHT! THIS IS SO COOL!" he hollered, his face the perfect picture of pure joy.

Together they skimmed over the rooftops of small neighborhoods, watching as the cars moved beneath them and disappear in their wake. The air had that crisp autumn flavor to it, but they were warm enough within the glow of the hat's magic. Daisy felt a bubbly excitement fill her up and soon she found herself taking a couple of swooping turns, skipping playfully off of zephyrs of cool wind.

"There's my school!" Nate said over the rush of air, pointing towards a squat building a few blocks away. They noticed a few kids at the playground – none of which seemed to notice the trio flying overhead. "How is it they can't see us?"

"We're flying through the air, and the first question you ask is why they can't see us?" Daisy laughed and circled the park before darting back up over the treetops. For the first time in a long time, Daisy was really enjoying that feeling of exhilaration that came with gliding through the air. She had loved it when she first learned how to, but after a couple of bad landings, she had changed her mind. She glanced back at Zora one more time and noticed that she had her eyes closed tight.

"Are you ok, Zora?" she said. "Don't be afraid. I've got you."

"Can we just get there, please!" Zora growled.

That second Daisy realized one small detail she had missed. "Guys, which way is the museum exactly?"

Zora's eyes shot open. "You don't know?! How you could shoot off into the air and not know where we're going?!"

"Just wait a minute. I'm pretty sure it's down 12th, that way…" Daisy glanced to her left and didn't notice the unfortunate group of Canadian geese that had just taken off from the park.

"DAISY!" Nate hollered, shifting his weight to her side, and the three of them barrel-rolled in a blur of feathers and excited honks, barely avoiding the flock, but speeding directly towards a stand of trees that stood like a wall of spikes in their path.

"NATE!" Zora screamed and shifted her weight, sending them spinning in the opposite direction, skimming the sidewalk inches from a small woman walking her Pekinese. Daisy tightened her grip on the children and took back control. She planted her feet against a light post as they sped by and pushed off hard, pulling up sharply into the sky. They were hundreds of feet up before she felt safe to stop and catch her breath. She took a moment to collect herself before looking down at Nate and Zora, awaiting their reactions.

"Sorry," said Daisy shakily.

"That…was…AWESOME!" Nate said. His shades sat crooked on his nose so Daisy could see the absolute glee in his eyes. "Let's do it again, this time with more barrel rolls!" Daisy couldn't have been happier to hear those words. She turned to Zora and found her reaction a bit less enthusiastic.

"Could we just get to the museum, already," she said nervously. She glanced down at her watch. "I'm not scared or anything, but it'll be lunchtime soon. Nate gets cranky when he misses lunch."

Through the fear and excitement, Daisy thought she saw the slightest hint of a smile sneak acrossed Zora's face, but it disappeared like an ice cube on a hot stove the moment she noticed Daisy smiling back. "We're almost there," Daisy replied. "I can see it from here." Sure enough, they could start to make out the top of the museum from their place in the sky and as she guided them down Nate kept making circular motions with his hand and mouthing the words "barrel roll." Daisy pretended not to notice.

The Hoskins Museum of Science and Industry wasn't what Daisy would consider the most fun of outing destinations, but the families and groups that milled about the place seem to be enjoying themselves. The austere interior of the building, obviously made back in a time when cold marble floors and high columned hallways were the architectural fashion, was now decorated with lively banners and posters asking museum-goers to "Experience the WONDER of history." There were dinosaur bones and playful dioramas, dusty mannequins wearing the garb of ancient Neanderthals, and a large bubble machine you could stand in to demonstrate the concept of surface tension. The bubble machine was, of course, Daisy's favorite exhibit, and she and Nate spent a lot of time putting it through its paces. Zora, however, wandered off to the Engineering Wing of the museum the moment they arrived, which made it difficult for Daisy to do her job. She could feel that familiar sensation of impending failure rising in her stomach. How was she supposed to impress this girl when not even flying seemed to do the trick? Something drastic was going to be necessary. Zora was special – Aunt Mizzy's critic note had said so, and Daisy was going to have to bring her A-game if she planned on finding out why.

"Your sister was really keen on seeing something in here," she said, watching as Nate once again encased himself in a giant bubble. "You wouldn't happen to know why?"

"Not sure," he said, smiling as the bubble popped and sprinkled soapy drops on his jacket sleeve. "But she's been talking about it for days, ever since she saw something about it on the news. I zone out when she gets too geeky though."

"Interesting. Well, let's go catch up with her. She shouldn't have to enjoy it alone," and together they walked in the direction they had last seen Zora heading.

The Engineering Wing was deep in the building behind two large doors, each with a banner hanging across it introducing the new Rathmore Exhibit of Invention and Ingenuity: 1926-1992. On the banner was a black and white photograph of a stern looking man in a dark suit. He had a handlebar mustache and long, steely gray hair, and his eyes seemed to follow Daisy as she approached the doors. She couldn't help but feel uneasy under his intense gaze.

"Creepy," Nate said, eloquently summing up her feelings precisely.

"Right! It's the eyes. They're following us."

"No wonder nobody's on this side of the building," Nate giggled. "– Ole' captain grumpy pants here is scaring them off."

"Imagine having to stand under that face all day," a guard grumbled. "I had a dream the other night he was trying to smother me in my sleep." Both Nate and the guard shuddered. "Anyway, haven't had much foot traffic on this side of the museum today so I was about to close the gallery up. You're welcome to come inside, though."

He helped them open the heavy doors, and they entered into the exhibit space. The large gallery was filled with a host of strange objects, from the chassis of a futuristic car with elaborate wings and large round windows, to tall glass cases filled with models of twisting structures and bizarre clockworks inside. Along the walls were large black and white photos of E.W. Rathmore at building sites and archeological digs and one of him standing in front of the building that was now the Hoskin's Museum. The centerpiece of the gallery, however, were five suits of armor standing silently in the middle of the room. Their design was most peculiar – like that of samurai warriors but made completely of a pewter-looking iron. Each wore a helmet and mask fashioned into a menacing face and carried a large metal staff in their hands as if they were standing at attention and awaiting orders.

"Fascinating, aren't they?" said Zora as she walked quietly up beside Daisy.

"Yeah…fascinating was exactly what I was thinking," she replied, doing her best to sound intellectual and worldly like Stephanie had suggested. "Your brother tells me you've been excited to see all this. I hope you found everything you were looking for."

"Not quite, but it hasn't been a total loss." Zora removed a small pad from her bag and jotted down a few notes. "These designs are beautiful, and far more advanced than most people would think. E.W. Rathmore was an amazing man – brilliant even. Have you ever heard of him?"

Daisy lifted her chin a bit. "History was never my best subject," she replied.

"Well, that's not a big surprise," said Zora with a smirk. "Not a lot was known about the man until very recently. Not long after the turn of the century, Elias Wilson Rathmore became an inventor and developer here in the Pacific Northwest and settled in Portland. He was a genius, but eccentric and secretive. He's credited with a number of astonishing inventions, but he always kept his contributions anonymous or at least understated. Even this exhibit only shows a fraction of the things he did. It's just incredible."

Daisy nodded in agreement, "Incredible. Sure – but what's with these grim looking guys?" and pointed to the suits of armor.

"Rathmore called them the Five Brothers," Zora said, looking at them with admiration. "He kept them in his study, standing in each corner and one behind his desk to intimidate his business partners."

"Really?" Daisy took a long look at their hollow eyepieces. "I'm sure that worked perfectly."

"I'm sure it did. Intimidation is an important tool," Zora said. "It keeps people...honest."

"You don't need an army of metal soldiers to keep people honest."

Nate shot forward. "That's right!" he said, straightening his jacket. "That's why you have a little brother."

Daisy shook her head. "I know you guys just met me, but trust me when I tell you that intimidating people doesn't really inspire trust."

Zora crossed her arms. "So, Ms. Kidd, what would you suggest?"

Here's your chance. Daisy smiled, her eyes twinkling. "I think that inspiration works best." She quickly went to the door of the gallery and dragged a nearby bench up against the latch. Considering what she was planning, she didn't want any unexpected guests. She reached into her pocket and pulled out the shiny brass pocket watch, and set the dial to three minutes. She then closed her eyes, held a clear image in her mind, and activated the Splendid Machine.

Daisy felt the same electric sensation she'd felt at the lab, and heard the whirring sound of its inner workings spinning to life. She opened her eyes and looked down at the watch face with breathless anticipation – all the while noticing that Zora and Nathan were waiting to see what happens next. *Come'on, work,* she thought to herself, but in the next moment, she knew the instrument had done its job.

One of the suits of armor moved. With the groaning sound of metal on metal joints, the suit stood straight and properly stepped out from amongst its "brothers." It walked forward to Daisy, and with a stiff sweep of its arm, bowed and extended its hand. She glanced back at Zora and Nate, and both of them looked on with wide open mouths.

"What's going on?" Zora murmured with genuine surprise.

Daisy smiled. "This metal gentleman would like to dance." She curtsied to the iron soldier and said, "It would be my honor sir," then took its hand and began to waltz across the marble floor. The suit of armor was remarkably light on its feet, and although his grim mask showed no emotion, Daisy compensated by humming a light tune as they glided around the exhibits. It sounded like Swan Lake accompanied by the drum of large metal trash cans. No one else was in the exhibit space, and Daisy couldn't help but wish she had a larger audience for her big finale. With a graceful spin, the iron soldier lifted her into the air, catching her like a prima ballerina before returning Daisy to the ground. It then bowed deeply, as it had in the beginning.

"Thank you, dear," said Daisy, playfully swatting the armor on the shoulder. "That was very nice." She then turned to the children and curtsied as Nate broke out in applause.

"BRAVO!" he yelled, running up to examine Daisy and the armor. "That was the most incredible thing I've ever seen!" He couldn't take his eye off of the now silent iron figure, looking all over its body for signs of how the dance was accomplished. "You have to show me how you did that. Is it wires? There's got to be wires. WHERE ARE THE WIRES?"

"It's not a trick, Nathan," Zora finally said calmly, as she slowly walked forward, "it's real. Real magic, am I right?"

"Of course it is," Daisy said, a little put out that she wasn't more amazed. "I did fly you here earlier, so I assumed you knew that. I can do magic."

"Magic is just science that most people don't understand." Zora crossed her arms behind her back. "The flying was impressive, but I've accomplished zero gravity fields before. But this? How did you control the armor?"

Daisy knew she shouldn't show her the Splendid Machine, but something had to impress this girl. She pulled the watch out her pocket and held it aloft by its chain.

"This is just one of the wonderous items I have at my disposal. With it, I can make amazing, impossible things happen – with just the click of this button," she boasted. "Believe me now?"

Zora examined it as is spun slowly in lazy circles before her, the light catching so delicately off of its engraved surface. When she reached towards the watch, Daisy had an overwhelming urge to pull it away. Before she could act, Zora's finger lightly brushed across the face of the watch. In an instant, they both recoiled, feeling a wave of energy surge between them – as if the air in the space between them had suddenly rushed out, vibrating their bodies like striking a tuning fork. The sensation only lasted a second, but when passed, Daisy noticed a bright glow emanating from just underneath Zora's shirt.

"That was…interesting," she said, quickly returning the watch to her coat pocket. "Are you ok, Zora?"

Zora checked herself, her hand gingerly checking the spot where the light had emanated from. "I'm fine," she said breathlessly, "but I didn't expect the feedback to be so…" She stopped mid sentence, her eyes going wide with surprise. "Uhm, Ms. Kidd, please tell me YOU are doing that."

"Doing what?" Daisy looked over at Nate, who was now slowly backing away from the suit of armor with a wary look. Daisy turned around and felt all the blood drain from her face. All five of the iron soldiers were now standing at attention, grabbing their long staves with grim purpose – red light burning in the hollows where eyes should have been. Slowly, they began to walk towards her and the kids with heavy, clanking footsteps.

"I don't know what you two did," said Nate in an ominous tone, "but these guys don't look like they want to dance."

BATTLE AND ULTIMATUMS

"**N**ATE, LOOK OUT!**" Zora screamed, reaching for her brother. The first iron soldier lunged for him as the rest came stomping towards her and Daisy, clanking and heaving their weapons as one. Nate barely dodged the gauntleted hand and scrambled underneath its legs.

"Look out for yourself!" He yelled as he came up beside Daisy. "Would one of you two please tell me what's happening? One minute these guys are sweet – now they're all stabby!"

"I don't know! Something went wrong with the watch." Daisy removed her bowler hat and reached in all the way up to her shoulder. She fumbled around inside as the soldiers stomped closer and closer. Finally, she pulled out a long black umbrella. "Get behind me, kids!" she said, holding it like it was a broadsword.

"Seriously! What are you supposed to do with that?" said Zora. "Those are real weapons in their hands, not water hoses."

Almost in response, the first suit of armor swung down its spear, missing Daisy's arm by mere inches. It attacked again, this time swinging low, and she parried the blow with the umbrella sending the iron soldier off balance, and it fell to the floor with a resounding crash.

"Ha! That actually worked!" Daisy laughed. She had basic combat training but had never put it use. She was elated to see that some of it had sunk in. "Take that, creepy!" Daisy yelled, but the victory was short-lived. The other iron soldiers quickly filled the space left by their fallen brother, bringing their weapons down on their targets in unison. Daisy barely had a second to open the umbrella, and a sudden blast of wind issued from it knocking their attackers back a few yards.

"What kind of umbrella is that?" said Nate. "I want one."

"Standard issue for nannies. Now run kids!"

"Run where?" Nate pointed towards the exit. "You blocked the door!"

Zora turned towards the end of the gallery where the chassis of the future-car sat. "There. We can hide behind it." It took the soldiers a moment to recover, which gave them only seconds to run around and past the exhibits. They skidded to a halt once the car was between them and the animated suits of armor.

"Ok, this isn't going the way I had hoped," Daisy said, breathing hard but trying her best to keep smiling. "The magic isn't supposed to work this way. Something… amplified the effect." She looked pointedly at Zora. "Something powerful."

Zora noticed the glance and pulled her coat closed, quickly tucking something into her satchel.

Without warning, they heard the sound of groaning metal, then the snapping of high tension wires. They turned to see a large model suspension bridge come soaring through the air, smashing into a thousand bits against the stone wall behind them. Amidst the crashing, Daisy heard a high pitched scream. She didn't realize it was her own voice until she saw the surprised look on the children's faces. Nate shook his head in disapproval.

"Please focus Ms. Kidd," Zora said. "Our problem now is that we need to get to and open that door." They all chanced a peek through one of the open windows of the car and saw that their attackers were blocking the way to the exit. Daisy heard someone drumming on it from the other side, even over the clanking of the advancing iron soldiers, but nobody was coming to their rescue.

"How do you suppose we're going to do that?"

"Since I don't think that umbrella is going to do the trick," Zora glance mockingly at Daisy's only weapon, "you're going to have to let me and Nate handle this." Zora opened her satchel and produced two leather gloves, each covered with various metal plates and apparatuses, and a brass ball about the size of a grapefruit etched with intricate grooves and circular shapes. "It's time for Ultra-Handball."

"Oh no," Nate grimaced, pointing at the items in his sister's hands. "First off, why do you even have those on you?"

"I thought we might have a minute to work on them today." Zora shrugged. "We are out."

"You said those weren't 'perfected' yet. You remember the last time we used something you hadn't 'perfected'…"

There was another deafening crash as the iron soldiers demolished another of the exhibit cases, sending glass and shrapnel spinning their way. The suits of armor were smashing their way closer.

"We don't have time – we're testing these in the field," she said and tossed a glove his way.

As Zora and Nate pulled them up, Daisy distinctly heard a revving sound, like a battery charging up. The brass ball immediately floated above Zora's outstretched hand, distorting the space around it. The ball moved and vibrated as if it were just waiting to shoot off. That's when Daisy felt it – magic! Zora Sparks had a wonderous item – one Daisy had never seen or even heard of before.

"Where did you get that?" she said, sounding more than a little awed.

"Not the time for questions, Ms. Kidd," Zora replied, waving off the comment.

"I don't care. What exactly are those supposed to do? Nothing dangerous, I hope," she said, the sound of authority returning to her voice. "You do realize that it's MY job to protect you."

"So then Ms. Kidd – do your job."

⁓⳨⁓

With that, Zora and Nate shot out from their cover, running to either side of the advancing soldiers. The Five Brothers took notice right away, but not in time. Once in position, Zora held out her hand.

"Ready?"

"Ready!" Nate replied.

The lead soldier turned as Zora wheeled her arm around like a baseball pitcher and slung the dark orb with all her might. With a CLANG! its helmet flew off, knocking it to the ground as the orb rocketed towards the ceiling. It hit a rafter, ricocheting towards the north wall, off the corner of another exhibit, and zoomed into Nathan's open hand.

"Nice!" he said, knuckling the ball and grinning from ear to ear, "but I can do better." Nate reared back and sent the orb sailing, but not at the soldiers. Instead, it ricocheted off the ground and smashed loudly into the soldier at the rear of the group. The orb smashed through its midsection and blasted out just under its shoulders, sending its arms and helmet flying off in three different directions.

"Nate, stop showing off!" Zora yelled. The orb bounced off walls and smashed through glass displays, gaining speed with each ricochet, until Zora dove and caught it again in her gloved hand. "Got it." When she looked up, a headless suit of armor loomed over her with its spear leveled at her nose. It was close enough that she could smell metal polish on its weapon, and a slight hint of ozone wafting from where the helmet used to sit. It drew back on the spear slowly, but as Zora prepared to throw the orb – something jumped in front of her. In a whirl of her red paisley skirt, Daisy flew past knocking the spear aside with her umbrella and grabbing the girl with her free hand.

"What are you doing?" Zora cried as she lifted from the ground, "I had everything under control!"

"Oh, shut up and let me save you," Daisy replied, dragging her clear.

Across the room, they both heard Nate call out. "Hey! How's about some help over here?" They turned to see him with his back to the wall as the three remaining soldiers closed in. One attacked and was met with an astounding kick to head, while the next was knocked back by a blindingly fast punch. Nate was a whirlwind, spinning and attacking like the hero out of a kung fu movie – but he could do little against their metal forms, and his wry smile was quickly turning to worry.

"We're coming!" said Daisy. She and Zora came running, hoping that some kind of plan might materialize.

"AS SOON AS POSSIBLE, PLEASE!" he yelled again, the soldiers surrounding him.

"I have an idea," Zora said, "Daisy, can your umbrella do that wind thing whenever you want?"

"Sure, but I don't think that it's going to do much good."

"Trust me, this will work." Zora's brow tightened in concentration as if she was doing complex calculations in her head. "We only have one shot, though, and you have to be ready...now!" Suddenly she took off towards the soldiers, pointing at a small gap between them. "Aim here!"

Daisy aimed the umbrella and opened it wide, sending a swirling coil of wind that slammed into the suits of armor. As it tore past, Zora jumped into the wind's path, shooting forward with amazing speed as she simultaneously hurled the orb at the wall ahead of her.

"NATE, DUCK!"

Daisy slammed the umbrella closed and Nate instantly dove for the ground, just as the orb hit right above where his head had been. It ricocheted to the left in a hail of stone and dust hitting the headless suit of armor in the chest, rebounding into the one across from it, caving in its breastplate, and sending the orb smashing into the third armor's mask. The last of the Five Brothers fell to the ground with a thunderous crash.

Zora lay at her brother's side as Daisy ran to them, her umbrella ready in case the suits moved again. But, just as she stood over them, the red glow within the armors slowly died away, and the scent of ozone dissipated.

"I think it's over," she said, letting out a sigh of relief. "Are you guys ok?" She hastily examining them for injuries, finding none.

Nate stood and dusted himself off. "Nate, duck? A little more warning next time, ok Zo," he said and smiled. He turned and kicked a gauntlet that lay at his feet. "What's up now, trash can? Your friends here have lost a little of their pep." They all looked down at the now motionless suits of armor.

Across the room, Daisy heard the doors into the gallery burst open. In walked a group of men in tailored suits. They wore very distinct white gloves and were dragging the wide-eyed security guard behind them. Lastly, there entered a tall, thin man wearing peculiar spectacles and carrying a golden-headed cane under his arm.

"Hello, Miss Kidd," Mr. Flint said in a low, cold voice. "I'm very much looking forward to your explanation for all of this."

⸻

Daisy felt the blood rush from her face. Mr. Flint, Hobbs, and no less than five other Daggers had just found her in the most awkward of situations. When she surveyed the room, taking in the damage and all out destruction that lay at her feet, she felt that oh so familiar queasy feeling in the pit of her stomach. The air was filled with concrete dust, and the floor was covered with shards of glass and stone, and while a few of the exhibits had survived unscathed, much of the room looked like a bomb had gone off between those walls.

"Funny story, sir. One I'm happy to explain," she said in barely a whisper, " You see…"

"Wait a second – who are you that she needs to explain anything?" Zora interrupted, stepping between them with her thin arms crossed. "If you work for the museum, I think you should be glad we weren't hurt. These exhibits weren't built very sturdily, were they Nate?"

"What? Oh yeah, they were really shoddy – and I'm sure that I could smell gas when we came in. Yeah, gas! This must have been some kind of gas leak!"

Mr. Flint approached Zora and looked down at her – unamused. "I think I'll let Ms. Kidd recount events if you don't mind. And as for who I am, Ms. Sparks, you might say I am a representative of the Department of Children's Services," he said in an ominous tone. "We've had issues with you and your brother in the past, and another incident can not be tolerated. I'm here to make sure that you are behaving yourselves, and that your caretaker is doing her job. Sadly, this is not the kind of environment I was hoping to find you in. Most disappointing."

Daisy noticed Zora's face drain of color.

"I can see you understand then. Good." Flint turned to his men. "We need readings on the room, and a cleanup crew immediately. Tell Porter this is a Level 5 priority."

"What about this guy, sir?" Hobbs said, eyeing the security guard with dark intent. "Should I let the Stewards will take care of his memory, or handle him in a more…permanent way?"

"Not necessary, Hobbs. I'll take care of this one." Mr. Flint tapped his cane against the ground, sending a wave rippling through the ground towards the cowering guard, who was instantly engulfed in bright light. When it died away, the security guard stood there with a confused look on his face.

"That should do the trick. Keep an eye on him to make sure the suggestion took. We don't want this unfortunate gentleman running off to tell tales, do we?"

"No, sir. We do not." Hobbs took the bewildered guard by the arm and led him out of the room, all the while the poor man babbled repeatedly to himself, "I just took a coffee break! Twenty minutes and there was gas explosion? It's not my fault."

When the gallery door closed, Mr. Flint returned his attention back to Daisy. "Ms. Kidd, could we have a word alone?" he said, motioning her away from the children.

"Stay here kids," she said and followed without question.

Once out of earshot, Mr. Flint voice turned low and icy. "Ms. Kidd, it would be disingenuous of me to say this is a surprise. Your first full day with these children, and you've already racked up a hefty toll of destruction. How exactly could something as incredibly foolhardy as this have happened?"

Daisy started to speak, but Flint held up his hand.

"It doesn't matter. Obviously, you are not ready for field work. I guess I will have to contact Mr. Porter about sending you back to the Stewards division."

"No sir, please! I promise this was just a coincidence!" The truth of the matter, Daisy didn't know exactly what had happened, but she knew that it had something to do with Zora and whatever she'd stuffed in her bag. But the message from her aunt's note stopped her from speaking – *The girl is important*. Tell no one. Daisy had to find a way to fix this without telling him what had happened.

"A coincidence? Really, Ms. Kidd, I'm about at the end of patience with you. Give me one reason that I shouldn't take your bowler and send you home right this second."

Daisy thought hard. "Because I'm…bonding with the children. Yeah! We've really been bonding."

Flint didn't seem too convinced. He stole a glance at Nate and Zora, to which Nate returned a large grin and a wave. "Bonding, you say. Have you made a determination on the girl yet?"

"No, but she's hard nut to crack. Trust issues, and all." Daisy leaned in and whispered. "If you take me away now, all that I've built with them will be lost, and you'll have to start from scratch."

Flint considered for a moment, tapping his thin finger against the side of cheek, then looked hard at Daisy. "I feel that I am wasting a great deal of patience on you, Ms. Kidd. However, you may have a point about the child, so you can continue. I will need regular reports. I'll need a determination on Ms. Sparks before the end of the year. That's two months. If you haven't done your job in the time allotted, measures will have to be taken."

"Measures?"

Mr. Flint leaned in towards Daisy. "Yes. Obviously, the girl is intelligent – maybe too intelligent. I might have to find her another 'situation' to better observe her. The home she's in now might not be the best place her. Are we clear?"

Daisy swallowed hard. "Yes, sir. Crystal clear. I don't think that will be necessary."

"Good. One more question – who's idea was it to come to this particular exhibit?"

Daisy paused then said, "Zora wanted to see it. Apparently, she's a fan of this Rathmore guy. Weird huh?"

"Yes. Weird indeed." With a click of his heels, Mr. Flint sharply turned and headed for the door. "Hopefully we won't have to have this conversation again, Ms. Kidd. It would be unfortunate for everyone involved."

Daisy, now alone in the demolished gallery with Zora and Nate, was filled with her own doubts and questions.

"Zora, you and I are going to have a long talk about this," she said. "About all of this, ok?"

"I think I saw that coming," she replied with an unreadable look on her face.

"Good. Come on guys, let's get out of here." When they headed for the exit, Nate ran up and took Daisy's hand and she noticed the look of pure contentment on his face.

"So where are we going tomorrow?" he asked, a hint of excitement in his voice.

Daisy couldn't help but laugh. "I don't know, sweetheart. Hopefully somewhere a little less dangerous."

Zora came up on her other side, and again Daisy saw a slight hint of a smile. "Can I make one suggestion?" she asked. "Can we PLEASE take the train. Hordes of fierce metal soldiers I can handle, but not your flying."

Dinner was on the table by the time Teresa got home and the smell of baked ziti wafted pleasantly through the house. Daisy and the children were washed up and ready to eat. The fight at the museum had left them all pretty dirty, so washing up was more for Teresa's benefit. They had all decided that they would edit out some of the events of the day if their aunt asked. Daisy got the feeling that she was going to have to keep a good deal from Teresa when everything was said and done, but Zora and Nate seemed to take it all stride.

"You guys look like you've had a great day," Teresa said, dropping wearily into her seat. "And dinner's made, too. Daisy, I think I love you. Isn't she great kids?"

"Mmhmm!" Nate said through a mouthful of pasta. "She's the best."

"What about you, Zoe – looks like you're in good spirits. Anything cool happen today?" Teresa asked, turning to her niece. There was a long moment of silence where all that could be heard was the clink of forks against plates, everyone around the table waiting with bated breath. Finally, she looked up.

"It was pretty fun, I guess," she said, and took her plate to the sink. "Don't worry about the details."

Teresa tried to ignore the dismissal. "Oh. Well, as long as you had a good time," she said.

"We did." Zora took a long stretch. "It's getting late, so I'm off to bed. Thanks for dinner, Daisy. Good night."

When they heard the last of Zora's footsteps on the stairs, Nate turned to Daisy with a satisfied grin on his face. "Look at that. I think she likes you."

"How can you tell?"

"Oh trust me, you'd know if she didn't," Teresa said glumly. "Take the win, Ms. Kidd. Just take the win."

ZORA SPARKS
THE LUMINARY

THE SECRET SANCTUM

Daisy had a hard time getting to sleep that night. The room Teresa had made up for her was very nice, with a large bed and fine furnishings, but the space still felt foreign – like staying at a nice hotel far away from the familiarity of home. Maybe it was the way the moonlight came through her open window, falling at strange angles across the striped wallpaper, or maybe it was the smell of lilac in the fabric softener in the sheets, or possibly even the way the quilt felt heavy on her chest. Whatever it was, her thoughts would not stop racing, and that uncomfortable feeling kept her eyes from ever quite closing long enough for sweet sleep to find its way in.

Eventually, she gave up and decided to stare at the ceiling instead, and when that proved fruitless, she got up and walked quietly down the hall to the bathroom to get a drink of water. As she filled her glass, she caught a glimpse of her own concerned reflection looking back at her from the mirror, brows closely knit in concentration. Something was nagging at her, and she knew exactly what it was.

What was that glowing object in Zora's bag? The thought was like a splinter – stinging, and just far enough under the surface that she couldn't help but pick at it. Daisy couldn't fathom what this peculiar girl could possess that would be powerful enough to effect the watch she had borrowed from Johann, let alone where she could have gotten her hands on it. Add to that her strange gloves and orb, plus her little brother Nathan and his uncanny abilities (she still hadn't figured him out in the least,) all proved that Zora Sparks possessed knowledge far beyond that of any Adept Daisy had ever heard of, and now she was her responsibility.

"You couldn't have written that on your note, could you Aunt Mizzy?" she moaned to herself.

She walked back to her room, pondering the mysteries of her new charge, and what her next move should be. Once inside, she sat the glass of water on the nightstand beside her bowler.

"We need to have a conversation, Ms. Kidd," a voice said from the shadows.

Daisy spun around. She reached inside her bowler, pulled out her umbrella, and pointed it threateningly at her unexpected guest.

"Wait a sec! It's me, calm down."

Daisy squinted, waiting for her eyes to adjust. There in a dark corner of the room sat Zora in her robe and pajamas, legs crossed beneath her and slowly drumming on the arms of her chair.

"Seriously!" Daisy said breathlessly, "Why do you have to sneak up on me? As if today wasn't enough of a shock to my system." She shoved the umbrella back into the bowler and sat down on the edge of the bed.

Zora leaned forward. "I just wanted to talk. You're the one that pulled a weapon on me."

"I'd hardly call that a weapon. Besides, what are you doing skulking around in the shadows at this time of night?"

"I wasn't skulking," Zora replied with a bit of a pout. "I never skulk. I was waiting for you."

"How long have you been there?"

Zora shook her head, "I came in after you went to the bathroom. Stop being so paranoid." She got up from her chair and walked to within an arm's length of the bed. "Everything that happened today, flying and the trip to the museum, was amazing, to say the least."

"Thanks! Amazing is my job," Daisy said feeling her heart swell with pride.

Zora took a step closer. "You aren't normal, are you?"

Daisy was taken aback. "Define normal?"

"You know what I mean! Take that hat, for instance. It's way bigger on the inside, and it made us fly. Those are things that a regular 17-year old nanny can't do."

Daisy rested her chin in her hands and blew a stray curl away from her eyes. "I guess not," she said, crestfallen. "Sheesh! You're supposed to figure it out, I get that. You're not just some little kid – but come on, you could have given me more than a day. Would it have killed you to throw out a couple 'oohs' and 'ahs!' Kids are supposed to be a little more amazed at magic. Accepting, yes, but still amazed."

Zora stood straight, her arms clasped behind her back. "I'm not your average kid," she said, her tone matter-of-fact, "and I'm not going to pretend I'm amazed if I'm not. I don't appreciate lies, and I've had enough adults try to lie to me before. They think because I'm twelve that I don't understand what it means to be deceived. Until I know what's going on with you, this arrangement isn't going to work."

Daisy couldn't help but agree. Zora was way more mature than the children she had previously encountered, and way more intelligent. It was like talking to a miniature adult, but not quite. The regular tactics were never going to work with her. Suddenly, Daisy knew that she was going to have to go a different route: honesty.

"Look, you and I may have gotten off to a bad start," she said, sitting up. "And you're right, I guess I'm not 'normal.' I'm different – like you, and like you, I can do things that most people think are impossible. In fact, that is what the people I work for sent me to help you with, but I am new to this. That doesn't mean I don't know a thing or two. One thing I can tell you for sure is that I'm here to help you and Nathan, and you can trust me."

Zora gave her a skeptical smirk. "Really," she said. "Prove it."

Prove it? Daisy looked around, forcing her brain to come up with something. Eventually, she pulled her bowler off the nightstand and slowly handed it to Zora.

"This is against the rules, but I guess there isn't any reason to keep it from you now," Daisy said. "My hat is standard issue for someone like me. Take a look."

Zora reached out and took the bowler and turned it around in her hands, examining it from each angle, then inside. What she saw took her breath away for a moment. Inside the bowler was a deep space almost the size of the room they were standing in. It was filled with a purplish light that seemed to twinkle and glow like starlight in soft focus, shifting ever so slightly with each turn of the hat. In that gossamer space floated an array of amazing instruments, each one more bizarre than the next, reflecting the light playfully off their burnished surfaces.

"This is impossible," Zora said. "You've attached a stable pocket universe inside of a hat?"

"It's magic! Seriously, can we just call it magic?" Daisy grumbled.

"Alright – a 'magic' pocket universe. Incredible! I've read the theories, but I never imagined it was possible. This is brilliant!"

Just then, Daisy saw her first true smile warm Zora's face, and a sparkle of delight glimmer off her big brown eyes. For the first time since she'd met, Daisy saw the excited child inside of Zora.

"Thanks, I guess," she said, "but I can't take credit. I'm just trained to use the stuff."

"Stuff? You have more?" said Zora, excitement in her voice.

"Oh wait, not so fast," Daisy said, grinning deviously. "Trust is a two-way street, kiddo. I shared a secret with you, now you share one with me."

"One secret?" Zora asked.

"Yes, but make it a good one."

Daisy noticed the look of indecision on Zora's face, but after a second or two, she nodded her head in agreement.

"Get your robe and follow me," she said, turning towards the door. "And don't forget your hat."

The rest of house was dark as they quietly made their way past Nate and Teresa's rooms, down the steps, and into the kitchen. There was a door in the corner of the room which Daisy assumed led to a closet or pantry, but when Zora opened it all she could see was darkness.

"The basement?" Daisy asked. "Aren't there spiders down here?"

"Yes, of course. It is a basement after all," Zora replied. "You scared?"

Daisy didn't like spiders or anything creepy and crawly for that matter. But, since she didn't want to lose any credit with Zora, she pushed away the thoughts of webs and spindly legs from her mind. Together the went down the narrow steps and into the gloomy space below. The air smelled of damp and dust once they reached the bottom.

Zora didn't turn on any lights but made her way deftly through the clutter of boxes, tools, and stacks of old newspapers until she stood at the far wall. Daisy's eyes were still adjusting, but she found her hearing had already become acuter. She could just make out the sound of a series of taps against the bricks before there was a quick sliding sound of stone on stone, and before them appeared a light. The wall had swung inward revealing another short flight of steps.

"You can't tell anyone about what I'm about to show you," Zora said. "Promise."

"Cross my heart," Daisy said, holding up her hand like a girl scout.

"No. Really promise." Zora said again, her voice full of deep meaning.

Daisy looked her in her eyes and nodded, matching her seriousness. "Yes. I really promise."

Zora seemed skeptical but still lead the way down. When they reached the bottom landing, Daisy felt her breath catch in her throat with amazement. In a space slightly larger than the basement they had just left, lay the most elaborate room she had ever seen. It looked like a cross between a second-hand antique shop and a mad scientist's lair. All around the room were half completed contraptions; from flying machines made with old copper pipes and bicycle parts, to jetpacks constructed from pre-World War I cappuccino machines, and an array of straps, brass gauges, and lots and lots of gears. The air was slightly stale, but had a copper tang to it, like the smell of machine oil and worked leather. It was so familiar that Daisy instantly knew what this place was. This was Zora's workshop.

"Welcome to the Secret Sanctum," she said proudly, stepping into the glow of the hundred thousand Christmas lights she had strung along the ceiling and walls. "Wait a second while I make it safe to come down."

"Safe?" Daisy asked as Zora jumped the last three steps.

"Yeah. From the booby traps, silly," Zora replied, as if it were strange she had to explain. She disappeared behind a stand of shelves for a moment and Daisy heard a whirring sound, followed by a sharp click. Zora reappeared with an impressive grin. "It's ok to come down now."

Daisy tested the steps with the tip of her slipper, and when no boulders fell or blades flew, she descended the rest of way into the workshop. The room was made of up of tall shelves covered in parts and abandoned projects, but with worn rugs laid throughout to cover the rough stone floor. Although the space was constructed of cast out items, like someone had raided a Salvation Army, it was very clean and orderly. Daisy walked amongst the objects for a few moments, taking in the advanced level of craft in each one. Some projects looked almost finished, while others appeared to have been abandoned early in their construction. She was walking past what appeared to be copper plated battle pants when Daisy noticed something sitting hidden behind a pile of extra parts. She moved the odds and ends aside to reveal a little copper bird, about the size of the palm of her hand. Its eyes were made of blue glass, while its wings were constructed of thin pieces of colored paper, intricately held together with wire. It was incredibly beautiful – a clockwork creature made that looked like a stain glass window come to life. When Daisy touched it, she felt a familiar tingle in the tips of her fingers, and the little bird blinked its eyes! It spread its rainbow colored wings and lifted off from Daisy's hand, flying in silent, graceful circles through the aisles formed by the shelving. She followed it for a few seconds, and eventually made its way to a well-lit work table on the other side of the room, where Zora caught it in mid air. She held the bird delicately in her hand, and for a second a look of melancholy came over her.

"It's lovely," Daisy said and smiled.

Zora nodded. "Thanks. I made him when I was really little. Before Nate was born, he was my only real friend. He'd follow me everywhere – I don't think I ever won a single game of hide-and-seek." The bird preened its wings and made a metallic cooing sound as it rubbed its beak against her thumb. "His name is Kuli. It means 'friend' in ancient Sumerian – my mom named him. She used to tell me that I was born to build stuff, but this was the first thing I made that was…special. She thought he was amazing." She ran her fingers over the delicate wings, then sat him gently down on the table.

"Making something like Kuli is an amazing feat," Daisy said.

Zora didn't seem convinced. "I've moved on to more useful things these days. Sometimes they work – most of the time they don't, but I keep trying to figure out why." She looked at the bird for a moment longer, then swiveled her chair around. "So, what do you think?" she said, spreading her arms. "Does this count as a worthy secret?"

Daisy had a hard time finding the words to capture her complete and utter astonishment. Zora was truly an Adept – and not only could she use wonderous items, but she could make them too – a skill thought lost by the Laurel Society for a century. All she could manage to say was, "Yep. This would do it."

Daisy walked over to the work table, which was covered with small tools and blueprints, and stood beside her. "How did you manage to find this place – not to mention get all of this stuff down here?"

"Oh, that. It didn't take too much, really. As soon as Nate and I moved in, I got some city plans from the library for this area."

"Really? City plans?" Daisy said incredulously.

"Yeah. Don't sound so surprised — I always get the plans when we move to a new place. Don't you?" said Zora. "Anyway, I was surprised to notice that Aunt Teresa's house was built over a series of old tunnels." She pointed to an old map she had tacked up above her table. "Everybody knows about the Shanghai Tunnels that were made around the turn of the century in downtown Portland, but there were lesser known networks built around the same time that run throughout the city. This room was used as a storage and maintenance room by the men who built those tunnels. Nate and I just added the door and the steps. It still needs some sprucing up, but it works for our needs."

"Nate knows about this place? What about Teresa?"

Zora glanced away. "She knows what she needs to. Satisfied?"

The whole thing sounded too convenient, but Daisy played along.

"So, I've shared something big with you. It's your turn again." Zora held out her hand. "I want to see that watch of yours."

Daisy leaned back a bit. She had the Splendid Machine in the pocket of her robe, but since the last time she had used it had almost turned into a massacre, she had been reluctant to handle the watch too much. "Sorry shorty," she said, waving Zora off. "It doesn't exactly belong to me. I sort of…borrowed it, so I can't just hand it out willy-nilly. Think of something else."

"Fine then, let me see your hat again."

Daisy reluctantly handed over the bowler, which Zora took and sat on a stand in the middle of her work bench. She pulled on her goggles (which Daisy only now noticed were in Zora's pajama pocket) and pulled a long thin instrument from a drawer and began to examine the hat. Each touch from the silver tool gave off a small burst of light that twinkled in the air for a second before dissipating. With each prod, she wrote something down in a small red-leather journal which was filled with notations, equations, and intricately documented sketches.

"There is no way this should work," Zora kept repeating to herself. "For all intents and purposes, this hat shouldn't exist. The mechanisms inside are beyond anything I've ever even imagined. Where is the flight apparatus?"

"In my coat. It's magic thread."

Zora laughed. "Seriously?"

"It is!" Daisy said, snatching her bowler back. "Is it so hard for you to believe that it's magic?" It felt strange having the girl poke and prod at bits of her world so cynically. She sat the hat on the table just out of Zora's reach.

"Magic doesn't exist, Ms. Kidd," said Zora, removing her goggles. "It's just science that people don't understand yet, like I said before."

"Well, you're wrong, miss know-it-all. Magic is real, and it's everywhere. It's in every drop of spring rain, and every fall leaf still clinging to the tree," Daisy said, feeling her face flush red. "Magic comes from every creative thought or feeling, every idea and every moment of pure wonder, and just because you can't see it doesn't mean that isn't there."

Daisy saw a small bowl on the table containing a pile of silver nuts and screws. She took it, poured the contents into her hand, and before Zora could stop her, she threw them into the air. Daisy focused, and instantly the nuts and screws began to swirl around in a whirling typhoon of metal, shimmering and twisting like a hollow in the air.

Zora looked in astonishment. "How is that even possible," she said, the shock evident in her voice. "You're not even using the hat!" She reached out to touch them, but just as quickly as they had begun to float, they nuts and screws fell clattering to the ground.

Daisy smiled sheepishly. "That was magic. Wild magic, mind you, but magic nonetheless. It has the ability to shift the very fabric of reality for a short while, but that kind of power is unpredictable; sometimes even dangerous. You never know how powerful the effect will be, or how long it will last. That is why I use that hat, and the tools inside. They were built using the Wonderous Science, which is how we make magic work for us safely."

Zora got quiet when she heard those words. "The Wonderous Science?" she said, letting it roll slowly off her tongue, like a melodious and foreign phrase. "What's that supposed to mean?"

"Imagine that all the rules of the universe weren't rules at all, but more like suggestions – and for some people, those suggestions could be bent, or even ignored. That is what the Wonderous Science is – a way to bend the natural laws of the universe, but without the pesky issues of wild magic, like spontaneous combustion."

"Does that happen a lot?" Zora smirked.

"More than you would think," Daisy replied plainly.

Zora sat in quiet thought for a second, pondering the possibilities before speaking. "Bend the rules, huh?" she said, "Say like gravity for instance? That's what you were doing when you flew us to the museum."

"Yes, like when I flew you to the museum," Daisy flipped the hat in hand and sat it on her head. "To be completely honest, I'm just getting the hang of that. You see, the wonderous items I carry can be tricky to operate. They are affected by your emotions – if you are scared, or angry, the end results can be pretty…unpleasant."

Zora's brow furrowed in concentration. "You mean like what happened at the museum with the suits of armor," she said under her breath, her mind obviously working through some kind of inner calculations.

"Right again, but that time was a little different. I think that something affected the watch – something you were carrying in your bag."

Zora looked up, her look of concentration replaced with angered annoyance. "Oh really," she said. It sounded more like a threat than a question. "What exactly do you mean?"

"I was hoping you would tell me," Daisy replied, the slight lilt of hope in her voice. There was a moment of silence between them that seemed to last forever, ticking by with a significant weight and importance that was reflected on both of their faces. Daisy was about to speak again when Zora slowly pulled on a thin silver chain that hung around her neck, revealing a round disk from the front of her nightshirt. No – not a disk. A gear.

"What is that?" Daisy said, reaching forward. Just as her hand was an inch away, the gear pulsed with a golden light that crept across its surface in lines of intricate symbols. She felt a force pushing against her, like two magnets repelling one another, and before she had a chance to examine the artifact, Zora quickly replaced the gear down the front of her shirt.

"Something my mom gave me. Something to keep us safe." Zora sat straight on her stool, arms crossed. "I'm not sure I want to talk about this just yet, Ms. Kidd." Her voice had a frosty tone to it, but under that cool demeanor, Daisy thought she saw a hint of fear in the young girl's eyes. It felt like she had pushed the sharing just a bit too far.

"Ok, ok, I get it – we're just getting to know each other. You don't have to tell me now if you don't want to, but eventually I hope you learn to trust me. This is all a lot to take in. Just know that I want to protect you if I can, and maybe even help you understand your abilities a little better." Daisy turned her hat in her hand. "Believe me, I understand a little bit of what you are going through. For instance, I have a foster parent too. An aunt."

Zora considered that for a second. "Really? You're not just saying that too, I don't know, to form some kind of 'bond' with me?"

"Never. I try my best not to lie. You and I aren't quite as different as you might think. Trusting people can be hard, but nobody can make it through this life alone." Daisy moved a step closer. "If you'd like, I could tell you a little more of what I know."

"About the Wonderous Science?" Zora said, thawing just a little. There was even a hint of excitement.

"Yeah. We could keep each other's secrets. What do you say?"

Zora considered for a moment, tapping her thin finger against her lip. When she came to her decision, she squared her shoulders and said, "That sounds possible, but I have conditions." Daisy nodded eagerly, and Zora continued. "Number one, Nathan and my aunt don't have to know about any of this – not until I say. My brother already is in this stuff too deep as it is."

"Agreed."

"Number two, if I think this is getting weird, or should I say 'weirder,' you have to leave. No questions."

Daisy hesitated, but when she saw the stony resolve in the girl, she grudgingly agreed.

"Last but not least, you have to promise to be honest with me, which starts with you dropping the prim and proper act."

That caught Daisy off guard. "Act huh? Was I that obvious?"

Zora smiled. "It's kind of ridiculous really. Way too sweet. I kept waiting for woodland creatures to come and do your chores for you."

"I was actually going for 'grand and extraordinary.' I've been told it works."

"Well, just plain Daisy is more than enough for me," Zora said.

That brought a grin to Daisy's face. "Just plain Daisy it is then," she replied.

DAISY KIDD
THE WARDEN

THE MASTER GEAR

"**A**re you sure this won't be a problem?" Daisy said, pulling on her coat and hat.

The family had spent most of the rainy Sunday afternoon with the children watching Nathan practice his crane style while the Kung-fu movie *Five Deadly Venoms* played in the background, and helping Zora put the finishing touches on her brother's secret birthday present. It was only a day away, and she had put the last week of work, a dozen or so melted down kitchen items (and a number of small explosions) into getting it just perfect. Daisy had provided what assistance she could, which wasn't much considering she had no idea what Zora was making. In the end, her contribution amounted to sharing as many of her wonderous items as she could for Zora to examine, making sure to keep her from taking them apart. It wasn't exactly something that was permitted, letting a child in care handle a wonderous item, but then again there was a gray area when it came to Adepts like Zora. She ended up spending hours with her in the basement lab trying her best to explain how a light manifesting coil worked, or a focused projection emitter and Daisy more than once wished she had paid more attention during her own training. This particular day had been so busy that she had lost track of the hour, and when time came for her to leave for her monthly check in at The Laurel House, Daisy was searching for any excuse not to go.

"Oh, it'll be fine," Teresa said from the den, "you've been working so hard the past few weeks. I just hate that you have to spend your time off doing paperwork.

Daisy nodded her head, remembering to play along with the little ruse she had created. "Yeah, it's pretty lame. The agency requires me to check in from time to time, and they prefer it be in person. I promise I'll only be gone for a couple of hours, and I'll be back in time to get dinner started."

"Go. We'll be fine, right kids?"

"Yep. All good!" Nathan barely registered the question as he performed a perfect roundhouse in the center of the living room, landing in a crouched position in sync with the character on the television screen. Zora, however, left her work on the living room table and approached Daisy at the door.

"So I'm assuming that you'll be talking with your bosses about us?" she asked plainly, standing with her hands on her hips.

"Yes, but nothing too personal. It's mostly about me and making sure that I'm giving you guys a good experience. Keeping you safe and stuff. They're pretty particular."

"That's fine I guess," Zora said, taking a large step forward and crossing her arms behind her back. "We've been in foster care long enough to know what these kinds of questions are about." Her voice took on a slightly more serious tone. "Just as long as you...do not tell them too much. I'm sure you understand." Teresa watched the conversation with a little confusion but was relieved by the smile of understanding on Daisy's face.

"Don't worry, I understand." Daisy pulled out her umbrella as she walked out into the gray day. She didn't like lying. Even small ones generally made her stomach fill with butterflies, and at this moment it was fluttering like crazy. It couldn't be helped, though. She had questions about Zora's artifact and there was only one person that she could think of who could answer them. Now she just had to get him to forgive her first.

Daisy landed on the roof of The Laurel House forty minutes later drenched to the bone. Funny how an umbrella was standard issue for Wardens, but did little to keep anyone dry in Oregon. When her heels touched down on the landing pad, they were met with the splash of rain puddles, to which she added the water draining from the edges of her pea coat. Flying was feeling more and more like an inconvenience, and she would have preferred to catch the train, but she didn't dare risk arriving like a Norm. Stephanie and Mr. Flint would never let her live it down. Luckily, Mr. Hawk was receiving Wardens today at the roof doorway with what looked like a solution to her wet predicament. As far as Stewards went, Mr. Hawk had to be the most peculiar of the bunch. He'd been there as long as Mr. Porter, but was not quite as enthusiastic about the job. He was known for grumbling his way through most tasks, particularly ones at the chapter house. The only times Daisy had seen him brighten up was when he was sent on etherea dispersal or magical incident clean ups. He'd get almost giddy during memory wipes, artifact captures, and anything with even the slightest hint of danger. Unfortunately, he wasn't doing any of that today, so he had his grouch-face on good and tight.

"It's really coming down, Ms. Kidd," he said glumly as she landed. Before she could speak, he aimed a burnished silver apparatus at her that looked somewhat like a 1950's style vacuum cleaner. There was a sharp rush of air, a sucking sound, and Daisy felt all of the rainwater pulled from her clothes. She couldn't help but think how glad she was that none of her clothes had gone with it!

"I think that's enough, Mr. Hawk!" she shouted over the whooshing, and he turned the machine off.

"Don't worry," he droned, "it's set to only get the water out. I learned my lesson last week – I still had it on the 'cloth' setting after doing the upstairs drapes. Ms. Lane and I had a bit of an awkward scene up here that I'm not planning on repeating."

Daisy blushed a little. "Yeah, awkward. So, I'm headed down. Talk to you later."

"Before you go," Mr. Hawk said with the hint of a smile, "any chance you've got something planned for today?"

"I'm not sure I follow," Daisy replied.

"You know. A horde of giant teddy bears, or liquid sidewalls – fun stuff! I have to admit, cleaning up your… incidents…is probably the highlight of my week."

She blushed even redder. "I guess we'll have to see," she said and shuffled to the stairs.

Daisy made her way down to the lobby, trying her best to not look like she was avoiding Mr. Flint's office.

She needed to get to the workshop before she made her report. "And besides," she thought aloud, "he can see the future. If he really wanted to talk with me right now he would have known I was coming," which felt like good logic.

When she reached the door to the workshop she tapped on the brass crest three times with her Laurel ring, just as she had seen Stephanie do before, but this time she was prepared for the spinning, lurching sensation that came after the gateway opened. She closed her eyes as she transversed the swirling, starry space and landed on the other side with only a slight stumble. When she opened them, she was once again standing in front of the workshop door, now in the stone hallway far from where she began. "I'm so getting canned for this," she mumbled. Straightening her coat and hat, Daisy walked inside.

The workshop was dark for the most part, although she could still see some wonderous items on the many shelves giving off some light of their own. Thankfully the room was empty this time of the evening but she did notice that one solitary light was still on in the far corner of the room. At the work-table sat a figure with an all too familiar stooped posture. She approached him quietly, watching as he worked – a series of instruments arranged in front of him hummed gently as he calibrated them meticulously. With each adjustment, he would make a note in his leather bound journal, which sat open, filled with his scribble drawings and precise script. For a moment Daisy was lost in the work, watching as her friend used his great skill and care on the aging magical apparatus. It didn't take him long to have it in perfect tune, filling the space with a pleasant hum like a plucked cello string. It was as she had always suspected; Johann Epstein was truly an artist.

"That sound is lovely," she whispered, and immediately Johann let out a yelp, falling from his stool in a jumble of tools and machine parts! The resounding crash was deafening.

"DAISY! WHAT ARE YOU DOING?" Johann yelled from the floor, more out of surprise than anger. "You could have given me a heart attack!" Daisy helped him up amid a million declarations of "I'm sorry!" and "Are you okay?" but his mood didn't seem to brighten. "Seriously, why are you here? I suspect you need something else from old trustworthy Joe, always willing to lend a hand or an experimental magical watch in a pinch." His speech was clipped and annoyed as he tried to return his work to its original pre-Daisy condition.

"Yes, but first I need to ask for something, and you have to give it to me."

He furrowed his brow. "What is that exactly?"

"Your forgiveness." Johann's face softened in response, so Daisy pushed on. "It was wrong of me to take the Splendid Machine, especially after you had originally offered to let me test it. I don't know why I took it. I guess I was nervous about my new placement. So much is riding on this, and I've been messing up so much lately. I suppose I just wanted something that would help me, you know, make a good first impression. Somehow even that backfired."

Johann smiled, running his fingers through his mess of curly hair. "You're not the only one that needs to impress someone, so I guess I can understand why you took the watch. There is a lot of pressure around here to produce results."

Daisy reached out and touched his hand, which elicited a blush from Johann. "So are we ok?"

Johann nodded his head, just as a quick look of realization came over him. "Wait a second – what do you mean it backfired?"

"That's another reason I came." Daisy pulled the Splendid Machine from her pocket and held it between her and Johann. "It was working fine at first, but…"

Johann took the watch delicately and held it under his work lamp, looking for damage or flaws. "But what? Did you tamper with the actuator gears of the dimensional timing? The slightest offset in the mechanism can be catastrophic."

"I didn't do anything to it," Daisy said, slumping down in the seat beside him. "When I first turned it on it was amazing! Effortless even. It was like it knew exactly what I wanted to do, and the magic just came to me." She could see the excitement in Johann's eyes as his inner Tinker took over.

"Excellent! What kind of magic did you enact? Was it something small, or complicated?"

"Small, I guess. I made a suit of armor do a little dance," she mimics the motion with her fingers across the worktable, elegant at first and then heavy and menacing. "That's when things got a little weird."

"A suit of armor? Where were you when this happened?"

"The Rathmore Exhibit at the museum," Daisy replied. "Zora, the girl I'm taking care of, really wanted to see it. While we were there, something…happened with the watch."

A look of concern came over him. "The army of armor soldiers, the ones the Stewards were called out to deal with, that was you? That was astounding! How on Earth did you manage it – or a better question might be why did you make them get all aggressive?"

Daisy couldn't help but feel even more embarrassed at this point. Apparently, everybody at the chapter house was talking about her colossal disaster. "It wasn't all my fault!" she said, "There were, um, extenuating circumstances that were completely beyond my control." She paused, remembering the warning of secrecy Aunt Mizzy had given her. Surely she didn't mean for her to keep secrets from Johann. She had known him since they were kids. If she could trust anyone with what was going on, it was him. As her thoughts raced, somehow Johann knew something was wrong.

"It's ok, Daisy. You don't have to explain anything to me." His smile was comforting, and Daisy felt her anxiety subside a bit.

"What if I were to tell you something," she said "something that you ABSOLUTELY had to keep to yourself? You can't tell Marco, or anyone else in the lab, and especially not Flint."

"What about your Aunt Mizzy?" Johann said with a smirk.

"When do you talk to her?"

"Uh, she comes by every now and then. I thought you knew."

"NO! Definitely not her!"

"Okay, okay. I get it - just between you and me."

She hesitated only a moment more before she blurted out, "Something Zora had with her amplified the effect of the watch. I'm not sure where she got it, but it was powerful."

"What was it?" Johann's eyebrows raised, his interest now peaked.

"It looked like a gear, but it had strange markings, and it gave off a glow - gold and purple all swirled together."

Johann suddenly went white as a sheet. "A gear you say?"

"Yes. About the size of a silver dollar, gold, and the etchings kind of like this." She took his pen and quickly scribbled some of the symbols she could remember. When she was done she noticed that her friend's hand was trembling. "What's the matter, Joe?"

Johann flipped furiously through his notebook, a frantic look in his eye that was a combination of excitement with more than a pinch of fear. When he found the page he was looking for, he turned and handed the book back to Daisy. "Is this what you saw?" he said, a slight tremble in his voice. Daisy looked down at the image that was meticulously drawn on the crisp, tan paper. It was the same object that Zora had shown her only days before, perfectly captured in crosshatched lines of ink, under which were written the words "The Master Gear" in a precise and fluid hand. "It's just a copy I made from the archives in New York, but I tried to get as much of the detail as I could."

Daisy nodded slowly. "Why do you have a picture of this?"

"That picture is why I'm here, Daisy – me and Marco. It's why Mr. Flint brought us to Portland, and why there has been so much secrecy. We are looking for this artifact, or more precisely, the artifact that it comes from." Johann looked over his shoulder into the darkened workshop and listened for movement or voices before continuing. "I'm not supposed to talk about this to anyone, and if Mr. Flint finds out that I've been blabbing he'll have my head, do you understand?" Daisy motioned locking her mouth tight. "Good. Because this may be the biggest discovery of the century. So, you know about The Waning?"

"I've read about it in a book before. *Secrets and Mysteries of the Wonderous World*. My aunt used to keep a copy in her office, but she said that most of it was bogus. She would always say 'Why would a secret society put their good secrets in a handy book anybody could read?'"

"For the most part she was right," Johann said, "since The Waning is common knowledge in our community, but the details are a closely held secret to most. In the 1920s, during the time most people in the world call The Great Depression, there was a diminishing of magic everywhere, and the levels of etherea dropped significantly throughout the world. But you see, it wasn't the first time something like that happened."

"It wasn't? Why haven't I heard about this?"

"The society doesn't like it to be common knowledge, not to mention that so much of our history has been lost or kept secret even to those of us that are a part of it. It's happened at least five times that we know about. This particular incident is special because we know why it happened, or more precisely 'who' brought it about – Elias Willard Rathmore." Johann flipped through a number of pages and landed on a well-rendered sketch of the man that looked exactly like the photograph Daisy had seen in the museum. "The world knew him as an innovator and engineer, but he was so much more. It was rumored that not only was he a practitioner, like you and me, but he was also an Adept. He could create wonderous items of incredible power the likes of which haven't been seen in decades."

As the new information settled on the surface of Daisy's mind, a question rose to the surface. *If the Laurel Society is just discovering this about Rathmore, is it just a coincidence that Zora was so interested in going to the exhibit?* It seemed unlikely, considering she had the Master Gear with her that day. Somehow, despite the fact she has had no connection with their world, Zora Sparks knew about Rathmore's magical secret. What else did she know?

"Do you know what this means?" Johann asked, pulling Daisy out of her own thoughts. He tapped on the drawing in the notebook. "It was whispered that he made an incredible discovery, one that he kept secret from the societies." He leaned in and his voice dropped to a whisper. "But there was an accident. A terrible accident that, some believe, brought about the Waning. Can you believe it? This may have been the catalyst for the Great Depression, and the years that followed. No one was ever able to find out what it was he did, but we've been studying the pieces that were discovered after his death. The Master Gear may be the key to uncovering one of the greatest mysteries of the last century. You have to bring it to the Society."

"No! Not an option." Daisy stood up angrily. "This girl has had enough taken from her, and enough grown ups betray her trust. I won't be one of them." Before she could turn to leave, Johann placed his hand gently on hers.

"Daisy, I'm sorry. I don't want to upset you, but I must." They stood there in the eerie quiet for a moment before he spoke again. "There are forces out there – dark forces that have worked against the Laurel Society for generations," Johann said with real concern in his eyes. "There have been incidents recently that the Society has tried to keep quiet. These forces would stop at nothing to get possession of something like this. Zora could be in real danger."

"Danger from whom?" Daisy pulled her hand away and put it back into her pocket. "Mr. Flint said something in his office the day he arrived. Something about troubles in other cities. What kind of 'forces' can't you tell me about?"

Johann looked away. "I'm not supposed to say. Please just trust me. I want to keep you and your charges safe."

"That's my job, Joe. She trusts me. If you can't tell me what we're up against, then I'll have to figure this out on my own."

"I wish I could help you more," Johann murmured, "but there's a lot I can't do since I can't leave the lab."

"Why can't you…" just then, Daisy heard footsteps, and she caught the sharp scent of peppermint and French perfume.

"Well, isn't this cozy." Stephanie's voice was low and even, but had a razor edge as she stepped into the halo of Johann's desk light. Marco stood at her side, his arms folded across this chest. "I'm sure you both can appreciate how surprising this is, finding you here together. Ms. Kidd understands that the labs are off limits to junior society members, and you Mr. Epstein know that it is strictly prohibited to discuss your work."

Oh no, she called me Ms. Kidd, Daisy thought. *That's never a good sign.*

"We were just catching up," she stammered, fumbling with her hat, "and Johann didn't even know I was coming. I was just at the office so I figured...I'm sorry, Ms. Love. We're both sorry." Johann nodded his head urgently, seeming to have lost the ability to speak.

"You might as well give them a break, Stephanie," Marco said, "it's not like we've never bent the rules a little." He gave her a sideways glance, and Stephanie's resolve seemed to soften.

"Fine I suppose. You're done with your check in and it's getting late, so I believe Ms. Kidd needs to be heading back to her charges, correct?"

Daisy agreed, and nodded a goodbye as she turned to leave. She got as far as the door when she felt Johann take her hand. "You forgot something," he said, slipping the watch gently into her grasp. He smiled nervously. "I think you're going to need this." Daisy smiled back and whispered a thank you.

As she reached for the doorknob, she heard Marco say, "How are those kids you're working with doing? No problems I hope?"

"Yeah. No problems at all," she said with as much confidence as she could muster.

As the starry expanse opened up before her, Daisy felt the butterflies begin to flutter in her stomach once again. However, it wasn't from traveling through folded space - it was because of what awaited her on the other side. The time for secrets was over.

JOHANN EPSTEIN
THE TINKER

INTERLUDE:
PLANS AND SHADOWS

When the three figures met again at Rathmore Cemetery, there was an obvious tension amongst them that could not be ignored.

"You assured me that this Ms. Kidd was perfect for our needs," Mr. Nail said, his voice quivering with rage. "She was supposed to have failed with the girl, and assured our plan would come to fruition. That has not been the case, and now the future has changed. I want the Master Gear, and not excuses. Rectify this quickly before things get out of hand."

"Everyone at the office knew about her lack of talent," Ms. Razor replied, her voice gaining in volume with each angry word. "Her success with the children has been mostly pure luck. Surely your visions showed you this? I've done my part!"

Mr. Hammer stepped forward casting his looming shadow over her, so menacing that she found herself moving back to avoid his gaze. "You'd be smart to watch your tone, lady," he said.

Mr. Nail raised his hand. "Not necessary, Mr. Hammer. I know what our next step should be. We need to speed up our timetable, and take more drastic measures." He looked off into the dark of the cemetery and the fog-shrouded headstones. "Prepare your men, Mr. Hammer. The time for subtlety is over."

Ms. Razor felt the blood drain from her face. "Now, sir? The Laurel Society will be alerted of our plan, not to mention the danger to the Warden and her charges."

"You should have thought of that before you failed to keep the situation in line, Ms. Razor." Mr. Nail said, as steady as stone. "Now, we'll leave it to the professionals."

AMAZO'S WORLD OF FUN

Nathan's birthday was a big event for the Sparks kids. Zora had been preparing for it for over a week, meticulously working on her secret gift and making sure that nothing would get in the way of her little brother having a great day. Eight years old is, as everyone knows, possibly the best year of your life - or at least that's what Nathan had proclaimed from the moment he woke up that morning. When Daisy returned to the house, Zora was already grabbing her coat to leave.

"You're late," she said as Daisy walked through the door. "We were supposed to be leaving at seven thirty. I could have sworn you had a watch." Zora turned and yelled upstairs, "Nate! Daisy's back. Get down here."

"I'm sorry, really," Daisy replied, "things ran a little long."

Zora examined her for a second, her intense gaze taking in every detail. "Something happened? You look a little, I don't know – concerned?" she asked pointedly.

"Nothing you need to be concerned about. Is everybody ready?"

"Almost. Nathan is distracted, as usual, and Teresa had to take a phone call." Zora turned and yelled up the stairs again. "Nathan, c'mon!" When he didn't answer, she squared her shoulders and belted out, "NATHANIEL ELIAS SPARKS! GET DOWN HERE RIGHT NOW! IT'S TIME TO GO!"

Nate came bounding down the stairs, flipped over the banister, and landed in a perfect crouch. "Ok, ok, I'm ready! Where's Teresa?" Almost on cue, their aunt hurried down the stairs as well, putting on her coat and carrying two suitcases.

"Daisy, I'm glad you're back," she said, avoiding the children's confused looks. Teresa pulled her aside. "Something has come up with work. I got a text from my boss in Dallas. He's there for the weekend with some clients and he needs me to fly out to assist. I know it's short notice, but can you handle the kids for a day or two?"

"Sure, that won't be a problem," Daisy replied. She lowered her voice a bit and leaned closer, "but is there any way you could make it to the party first? The kids really had their hearts set on it."

"I wish I could." Teresa fumbled with the handle of her suitcase, speaking low enough that her niece and nephew couldn't hear. "You need to understand, this is a big deal. I've been working for this hotel for three years, and this is the first time an opportunity like this has come up. I'm sure you can handle the party, right? Anyways, I'll be back on Sunday."

"You're sure?"

"It's not like they are going to miss me. They've got you." The words rushed out of Teresa.

Daisy stood astonished, searching for the right words to say in response. "That's not true, Teresa," was all she could think of. Then she noticed the look that came over Zora's face – a mixture of fury, sadness, and chilly resolve.

"You're leaving?" she said in a hushed and heavy tone. "I've been planning this for a week! You can't just leave."

"I'm so sorry sweetheart. I promise to make it up to you when I get back. We can go out and…" Before Teresa could finish, all of the lights in the room began to flicker violently, and suddenly exploded with a sharp crash, followed by the unsettling tinkling sound of broken bulb glass hitting the floor. They all stood in the silent dark that followed, the smell of ozone wafting in the awkward silence, and all of their attention on Zora.

"Have a good trip," she said in a cold, distant voice, then turned to leave. "I'll be waiting outside." After the door closed behind her, Nathan, Daisy, and Teresa were left looking at one another.

"Oh no. I just messed up, didn't I?" Teresa said.

"Don't Aunt T. That's just my sister gettin' crabby," Nate replied.

Teresa was speechless for a moment, then turned to Daisy. "Maybe this is a bad idea. I never know what to do with her when she gets like this, all dark and distant and looking at me like some kind of stranger. Should I say something to her?"

"Not right now!" Nate blurted out, stopping his aunt from following after her. "She just needs to get the grouchy out of her system."

"You don't want to miss your flight, either," Daisy said brightly and pulled Nate close. "The kids are in good hands, and this crazy guy is going to have a great birthday! You have nothing to worry about. Nope, you needn't worry about a thing."

Teresa smiled a half-hearted smile. "You said that already." She rummaged in her purse and removed two small objects; a package wrapped in blue ribbon, and a disposable cellphone, which she handed to Daisy. "Here, in case you need to get in touch. I remembered you don't have one. My number is programmed in."

"Right. Programmed in. Got it." Daisy looked grimly at the phone. She never had much luck with non-magical tools. She only hoped the phone wouldn't explode or anything if she used it.

Teresa turned to Nathan and handed him the wrapped package. "Here you go kiddo. Your mom and I used to have this tradition. When we got to spend birthdays together we would give each other one gift, no matter whose birthday it was. That way neither one of us felt left out. Now, I left your other gifts upstairs..."

"Did you get me the bo staff I asked you for!" Nathan asked, bouncing on the balls of his feet.

"Yeah, but I'm still not sure it's an appropriate present for a nine-year-old." She gave him a big hug, and kissed his forehead, "but this one is for you to give your sister."

Nathan turned the small package around in his hand. "Why don't you give it to her?"

"Considering what just happened, I think it will mean more coming from you," she replied sadly. "Have a happy birthday, little man." She kissed him again, then grabbed her suitcases again. "So where are you guys off to anyway?"

Nathan looked positively elated. "Only the most awesome place in the world. AMAZO'S WORLD OF FUN!"

Nathan could barely wait for Daisy to land when they arrived at the arcade. The place wasn't hard to find considering they could see the glowing neon signs from a mile away. Amazo's was connected to the Southside Mall between a family style Italian restaurant and ShoeWorld but was obviously the real central attraction of the area. Daisy and the kids landed on a secluded side of the parking lot to avoid being seen. She had to almost chase Nathan to the door, Zora following closely behind, though Daisy could see a lot of her excitement had been replaced with sulky angst. Once through the front door, Daisy was assaulted by the cavalcade of blaring sounds, flashing lights, and raucous children laughing and running pell-mell across the landscape of games and activities. The air had the spicy scent of pizza and overcooked popcorn, and the floor gave off a subtle sticky peel with each step. Amazo's was, without question, a kid's paradise.

They were greeted at the door by a lanky young man in an oversized red shirt, and across his chest were emblazoned the words "Amazo's Awesome Staff!" in blinking letters. He had a nametag that read, "Super Steve" but the bored looked on his pockmarked face said otherwise.

"Welcome to Amazo's World of Fun," he droned, "I'm Super Steve. Do you have a party reservation?"

Zora handed him a printed sheet of paper, and after quickly examining it, Steve said, "Follow me."

Daisy had never been to an arcade before and had to admit she was quite impressed. The large space was filled from floor to ceiling with games, banners, and flashing lights, all of which seem to draw the eye at every turn. Hordes of kids were jumping into ball pits, or springing through the air on enclosed trampolines, while others stuffed their faces with food at the tables or squealed with glee at the host of games that lined the aisles. Steve led them past all of this to their space, marked by a sign above the door that read "The Deluxe Party Experience." It was a smallish room with a table for eight, fronted by a large glass wall so you could see out into the arcade. Not very private, but Daisy got the feeling it wasn't really meant to be. Hanging above the table was a large banner adorned with colorful illustrations of characters that Daisy could only guess were Captain Amazo and friends, and large yellow text that read, "Happy Birthday Nathan!"

"Here you go," Steve said as they entered. Sitting in the middle of the table was rectangular sheet cake, covered in a rainbow of thick frosting, and an unlit candle shaped like a nine dead center. "Is this everybody in your group?" Zora glared at him in reply. "Oookay. Here are your game passes. Your food will be out in a little while, but feel free to take advantage of our salad bar." With that, he tiredly walked out towards the lobby amidst the roar of kids at play.

"You guys can wait for the food if you want," Nathan said excitedly. "Zora, you know where I'm headed."

"Now just hold on a second, mister," Daisy said, stopping him before he shot out of the party room, "I've never been here before. Which game are you going to use? Do you need, I don't know, quarters or something?"

Nathan took her hand and jokingly patted it. "Oh, you're so sweet. Quarters - ha! I've got credits on the card they gave me." He led her to the door and pointed. "That's where I'll be." At the far end of the arcade, Daisy could make out a line of kids waiting their turn on one of the largest games in the building. Two huge figures hovered above the crowd, one in blue armor and the other in red, staring menacingly at one another in fighting stances over the words "Dynamo Fists" in bold, flashing text. The game consisted of a large central screen position between two round pads on which the players did battle wearing immense, glowing gloves.

"That doesn't look very safe," Daisy said, a bit awed by the whole thing.

Nathan said, "Don't worry, D. I've played it loads of times." Before he walked out on the game floor, he turned and put the gift his aunt had given him into Daisy's hand, his usual cheery smiling fading. "Try to cheer her up," he whispered. "Sometimes I think that coming here means more to Zora than it does to me. This was a tradition when mom was around." His grin returned as if he'd remembered he was supposed to be happy, and he bounded off into the din of children's laughter.

Zora was sitting now, quietly writing in her red journal. She closed it as Daisy sat down beside her.

"Want some cake?" Zora said, reaching for a plastic knife.

"Shouldn't we wait for your brother?"

Zora rolled her eyes and cut a large piece. "He'll be out there forever. Besides, we're supposed to be having fun, right?" She handed the plate to Daisy and cut herself one as well and began to glumly eat.

"I'm sorry that your aunt couldn't make it, Zora. I know she really wanted to be here."

"Oh yeah," Zora didn't look away from her plate. "Well, she's not, is she? I guess it couldn't have been that important to her."

"I think it was. She knows that this was a tradition for you guys." Daisy said, poking at her cake with a small plastic fork. "You and Nathan don't talk about her much, but I know today is special to your mom too." Slowly, she slid the small package Nate had given her to Zora.

"What's this?"

"Just open it," Daisy replied. "It's from Nathan and your Aunt Teresa."

Zora pushed her plate away and picked up the gift. She ripped off the wrapping, and inside, smiling up at her, was a picture two young women in party hats, both of them no more than teenagers. One was Teresa, and the other looked just like Zora. "That's our mom," she whispered.

"She's very pretty," Daisy said gently.

"Mom loved this stuff. Cake, balloons, the whole thing." When she spoke, Zora sounded far away, as though somewhere in distant memory. "It was kind of cheesy, but she couldn't help herself. She was just that kind of person back then, always up for something fun. We didn't have a lot of money, and for the longest time it seemed like we were moving every couple of months, so birthdays became one of the only constants in our lives. She was always looking for a reason to celebrate; random holidays and stuff. One time we celebrated Walrus Day at the beach with walrus masks and everything."

"Walrus Day? Is that a real thing?"

"Apparently. It was just a reason to put on silly hats and eat cupcakes, but that's how she was. Her parties for us were something she always looked forward to." Zora wrapped her arms around herself. Daisy had never seen the girl look so vulnerable. She was always such a commanding presence, in her high-collared coat and tall leather boots, but underneath all that bravado she was still just a kid.

"She sounds like my kind of people," Daisy said. "Admit it, though, you loved those parties too."

"Yeah, I guess so. Really we just liked to see her happy. Every time we settled in a new town she would find the perfect places for us to go, just the three of us. Even after she started to get sick, she never missed one, even when it was hard for her to get out of bed."

Zora rubbed her eyes with the sleeve of her coat, then straightened. A look of cool determination came over her. "It doesn't matter anyways. I have a plan, and when I'm finished, we'll all be together again. No more Aunt Teresa, and no more foster care. I've almost figured it out." Zora pulled on the thin chain around her neck, lifting the Master Gear free from her shirt. "When I've found out how to use this, I'm going to make everything right."

Daisy could almost feel the power radiating from the artifact. How could she not have noticed it before, that thrum like a tiny heartbeat just beyond her senses? "Where did it come from, Zora, and why do you have it?" she said. "Until I showed up on your doorstep, you didn't even know anything about your powers, let alone the Wonderous Science, and yet here you are with what appears to be a very powerful artifact."

"Does it really matter? My mom gave it to me when they took her to the hospital, along with this," Zora said, tapping the red leather journal. "She told me to keep it safe, and that it was important. I knew there was power in it, maybe even enough to make mom better. I just have to figure out how it works."

"It could be dangerous to keep wearing that, Zora. You don't know where it came from or what it can do – or who else could be looking for it."

Before Daisy realized her slip of the tongue, Zora's hand shot across the table and grabbed her wrist. "What do you mean? Who else is looking for it?" The urgency in Zora's voice was almost frightening.

"I don't know!" Daisy tried to pull away, but the girl's grip was urgent. "I just have a feeling you aren't supposed to have it."

Zora was about to speak when suddenly the lights in the party room flickered. They both looked out into the arcade to see dozens of games and machines slowly powering down, leaving the entire arcade only lit by the red runner lights that lined the aisle.

"This can't be good," Daisy said. "I'm guessing this isn't supposed to happen?"

Zora stood quietly, listening to the questioning voices of the kids in the arcade starting to rise with panic. Then, at the rear of the arcade, they saw a flash of light, followed by a deafening series of crashes. After that, even in the dark Daisy and Zora could see figures running for the exit.

"Nathan!"

They both shot out of the party room, running towards the commotion. In the red light, they could see that most of the arcade patrons were already gone or running for the exit, driven out by the sound of destruction and the wafting smell of ozone. By the time Daisy and Zora reached the other side of the building where Dynamo Fists once stood, they both could see the gaping hole in the ceiling above. Four dark figures stood in the rubble, like brooding shadows cut out of the darkness. They were tall and broad-shouldered, each wearing black armored bodysuits. It was their faces, however, that were truly unnerving. Each wore a bone white mask with eyes that gave off an eerie, green glow.

One of the figures spoke. "I think we have something of yours," he said, his voice gravely and strangely altered. That's when Zora noticed her brother beside him, held tightly by the collar. "You have something that belongs to us. How about a trade?"

"Let him go!" Zora yelled, Daisy moving to stand between her and danger. The figure holding Nathan lifted his arm, and suddenly a roil of dark energy took shape, suffused with green and purple light that seemed to pop and sizzle within the mass of inky power as it formed into a blade over his hand. A point formed mere inches from Nathan's throat.

"You didn't say please," he growled. "Give us the Master Gear, young lady, before this gets terribly out of hand. The Blades of the Balance do not like waiting."

BLADES IN THE DARK

"Y ou make one wrong step, whoever you are, and I'll…"

"You'll do what, Ms. Kidd? Smack my hand and send me to bed?" the man said, his voice dripping with mockery. "I've heard a great deal of the Wardens' fabled fighting skills. They are legendary, and you do look like a truly fearsome sort."

He knows my name? He knows about the Society? But how? As Daisy stood defending Zora, young Nathan in the grip of the dark stranger, and her umbrella held before her like a saber, one thought kept coming to mind. *Why do Warden's carry umbrellas!?!* She couldn't shake the panicked thought. *I mean come on! What good is an umbrella!?!*

"My patience is wearing thin," the Blade said, twisting his weapon a bit to show the keen edge that had formed. "We already know you have the gear with you, Zora Sparks. We also are aware of its origins, and the power it represents. We're not leaving this place without it. I'm sure your mother would have wanted you to protect your brother instead of your little trinket."

Zora tried to push pass Daisy. "You don't know who you're messing with, black pajamas!" she said, swinging her fist in the air as she pulled her ultra-handball from her bag. "Daisy and I can take you and your buddies, no problem!"

"Dang skippy!" Nathan yelled. This drew piercing glances from the other Blades.

Daisy leaned close to Zora's ear and whispered. "I appreciate your confidence, but could we keep the taunting to a minimum?"

Summoning all her power, Daisy pointed the tip of the umbrella at the Blades and it glowed with an intense blue light. "I'm only going to say this once. By the authority of the Laurel Society, Guardians of Magic and Practitioners of the Wonderous Science, I order you to release the boy. It would be in your best interest to do it immediately. My superiors know we are in danger, and should be here shortly." Her voice rung out with impressive authority through the arcade.

"Well then," the Blade brought the tip of his weapon closer to Nathan's throat, "I guess we had better make this quick."

"WAIT!" Zora pushed past Daisy into the gap between them and the strangers. "I'll give it to you. I'll give you what you want – just don't hurt him." Zora looked scared, but more than that, Daisy could see something else in her eyes – concentration. It was as if she were working out some complex equation in her head.

"A very wise decision, Ms. Sparks," the Blade replied. He pushed Nathan out in front of him, but kept his hand tightly locked on the boy's collar.

Zora looked back over her shoulder at Daisy. It was hard to tell in the dark, but it almost looked like she gave her a quick wink before digging a package out of her pocket – one Daisy immediately recognized. Zora moved a little bit closer to the men, debris from the fallen ceiling crunching beneath her shoes, and when she as a few yards away she tossed the package at the Blade's feet. He stooped over, retrieved it, and tore the box open quickly. He reached in and removed two small bands. They were made of cheap metals, tin, and copper mostly, and were held together with a red ribbon that bore the words, "To the world's most annoying brother. Don't ever change."

"What is this, some kind of joke?" he said and threw the package to the ground.

"No, that's my little brother's birthday present," Zora said, giving Nathan a telling glance. "Pretty cool, huh? I based them after your favorite game."

Nathan's grin was positively electric. "Aww, Zoe! You're the best!"

"ENOUGH STALLING!" the Blade roared. He lifted his weapon and pointed it at Zora, the length of it crackling with swirling energy. "You are going to regret this, girl!" In his rage, he didn't notice his captive had picked up the discarded bracelets and was quickly putting them on. "You and your Warden will feel the power of the Balance, and beg for..."

CLANK! KA-BLAM!

Before he could finish, a gleaming metal fist smashed into his chest, sending him flying upwards through the hole in the ceiling with a glowing stream of light in his wake. The remaining three Blades looked on in shock. Nathan Sparks now stood in place of their leader, his fists raised and sporting a smile that seemed to say "time to play." He wore two large gauntlets of gleaming copper and steel, both literally pulsing with power.

"REAL DYNAMO FISTS! BEST. GIFT. EVER!!" he laughed, grabbing a nearby table and swinging it into the Blades like it was made of paper mache. "Now this is about to get interesting!"

Zora and Daisy leapt into the action, both racing towards Nathan, but the Blades hulking shadows were too fast. They moved like smoke stirred by a vicious wind, slicing through the table and coming for the boy.

Nathan met the first with a hard blow to the chest, the huge fists of his gauntlets sending out golden sparks with each contact. He moved like they weighed close to nothing, blocking the Blade's strange weapon while the other two came at him from either side. When the second attacked, he was smashed right in the face by Daisy's umbrella, trailing cool blue light in its sweeping arc. The third was caught off guard by Zora's glowing ball that ricocheted off his stomach, striking his chin.

"We need to get out of here!" Zora yelled as her ball returned to her hand. She grabbed Nate around his arm, dragging him off into the dimly lit arcade, Daisy close behind. Amazo's World of Fun was a wreck. Game machines lay on their sides in the aisles, some with their screens still flashing randomly in the darkness. In the labyrinth they formed, it was difficult to find the exit. Daisy pulled the children into the corner near the ski-ball games, and holding them both close, she quickly tapped the top right button off her coat. There was a hushed sound, like distant wind chimes, and in an instant, the three of them blended perfectly into the background.

"You have a cloaking device!" Zora whispered in surprise. "That would have been helpful to know."

"Quiet. It only works if you don't move around too much." Daisy whispered back, just as the Blades came into view. The closest one glanced in their direction, checking the shadows with his glowing green eyes. Daisy held her breath and felt the children tense up in her arms. After a moment that seemed to last forever, the Blade turned and moved on with his search.

"Do either of you know the way out of here?" she said in a hushed voice.

"They're blocking the exit now. We're trapped." Zora replied. "We could head back for the hole they made in the ceiling and you could fly us out."

"Those guys are too fast," Nathan said, "we should fight our way out!"

Daisy could hear the boy's fists tighten, the gauntlets giving off a slight, metallic scraping sound as he did. "Let's keep fighting as a last option, Nate," she said, gently squeezing his shoulder. She felt his tension ease slightly. "We just need to get some distance from them, not smash them to a pulp."

"I think I have just the thing." Zora rummaged in her bag, trying her best not to make any noise, and pulled out a triangular object about the size of a drink coaster, with dark glass nodes at its three points. "This is a doormaker. My own design. If this is the north facing the wall to the parking lot, and my calculations are correct, I can make a hole here for us to escape."

"Is that a bomb?" Daisy hissed in shock.

"It's not a bomb!" Zora hissed back.

"It's way cooler than a bomb," Nathan said, swelling with pride.

Daisy couldn't help but sigh. "Fine. Do it. As long as that thing isn't dangerous."

"I didn't say it wasn't dangerous." Zora placed the triangle on the wall and touched the three nodes. "Get ready, this is gonna be kind of loud," she said and activated the machine. Instantly, the nodes of the doormaker spread out, stretching to almost six feet across. There was a ripping sound, like peeling off duct tape, and the surface of the wall went totally black, rippling like the surface of a pool. "Oh no. I'm not sure that was supposed to happen."

"OVER THERE!" a grave voice called out. The Blades had found them!

"Keep them busy, you two. This takes a second to warm up," Zora yelled, making frantic adjustments to the doormaker.

"Now you tell us!" Daisy dashed forward, pulling out her umbrella just in time to block an oncoming Blade, while Nate's fists met another. The third dashed around them to grab Zora, but before he reached her the doormaker gave off a whirring sound that rose instantly to a high pitched whine.

"Grab onto something!" she yelled just as a force wave billowed off the wall like a great wind, knocking everyone to the floor. Once it passed, Zora, Nathan, and Daisy looked up to see a shimmering opening where there once was none.

"Go, kids, I'm right behind you," Daisy said as she pushed herself up, shoving her charges ahead of her. One of the fallen Blades grabbed at her jacket, slashing open her pocket. The cell phone Teresa gave her fell to the ground as she pulled away.

Once the kids were through the opening, she followed. Moving through the doormaker was an odd sensation – like walking through a space filled with thick and invisible Jello. On the other side, Daisy could see moonlight just beyond the cloud cover, and the darkened mall parking lot behind Amazo's World of Fun stretched out before them. "Quick, close the door before…"

Just then, one of their pursuer's weapons pushed through the gap, instantly changing from a thin blade into a gnarled claw, reaching and grasping at Zora's neck and shoulders. The girl was caught off guard, but Daisy was not. She swept her umbrella down hard in a blazing arch, and watched it explode on contact with the claw just as the triangular doorway collapsed in on itself. There was a flash, and the Blade's severed weapon fell to the ground. What remained of the claw was a pile of black dust that still crackled with green and purple light.

Nate kneeled down for a closer look. "Hey, this stuff smells like licorice."

"Be careful, you nut," Zora said, and popped him on the back of the head. She reached into her bag and removed a small, glass mason jar. "You don't know what that stuff is made of."

"It's not moving anymore," he said as he backed away. "It's probably not dangerous, right?"

Zora scooped it up into the jar and quickly stashed it away.

"Does anyone want to talk about how awesome I was back there?" Nathan asked.

Daisy looked down at the black polished handle of her umbrella, still smoldering. "Let's get out of here first," she said and grabbed both of their hands. "But before it gets away from me…happy birthday, Nathan." With that, she kicked off the ground and they sped into the moon lit night.

⸻

Daisy flew some miles away and descended into a small park in an unfamiliar neighborhood. Just beyond the tree tops, she could see the lights of Portland, the city feeling somehow cold and foreboding all of a sudden. The park was mostly benches and tables, with some playground equipment not too far off. A slight but rising fog filled the dark corners of a wooded area in the distance. When their feet touched the ground, Zora quickly pulled away, grabbing Nathan.

"You need to take us home. Right. Now," she said. "I don't know what you've gotten us into, and I don't care. You made me a promise that if things got too weird then you'd go."

"I know," Daisy replied, "but you and your brother are in danger, and I have to keep you safe."

"So why don't you call your 'super secret organization' for help?" Nathan said, drawing stares from his sister and Daisy. He shrugged sheepishly. "What? I've been paying attention. Can't they come and get us?"

Daisy sat down at a picnic table. She removed her hat and ran her fingers through her hair, trying to give herself a moment to put her thoughts together. "It's a little hard to explain, but I'm not sure if calling them would be the best idea right now," she said. "There are things about you guys, about all of this, that might cause us some problems. Things I'm not supposed to tell you."

Zora stepped up to her and put her hand on Daisy's shoulder. "I think the time for secrets is over, don't you?" she said. Gone was anger and distrust from her voice replaced with something that Daisy could only describe as compassion.

Daisy noticed a light flashing in her pocket, and she fumbled to pull her compact out. She snapped it open, and Stephanie's angry face appeared.

"Ms. Kidd, what is the meaning of this?" she said, annoyed and impatient. "I have reports here from the Stewards that you and your charges were part of another Level 5 magical event, in front of non-practitioners, endangering the children and the general public! I need your location and an explanation this instant!"

Daisy could feel all of the blood drain from her face and hands, and any words she might have had to say were permanently stuck in her impossibly dry throat, never to escape. She did, however, manage a few sputters, "Stephanie – I can explain – it's not what you…"

"Ms. Kidd! This is a catastrophe of epic proportions. I put my neck out for you with Mr. Flint, and this is how you repay me? I knew you were a bit of a flake, but this is beyond anything I ever expected. Do you have anything to say? Well, do you?" Stephanie Love's voice was more of a growl this time, causing Daisy's lip to quiver just a bit. Before she could speak, Zora took the compact from her hands.

"Who is this?" Zora said in her most defiant tone.

"Ms. Love, Warden of the Laurel Society. Who are you?"

"Zora. Zora Sparks. Look we aren't done talking to. Daisy, so you'll have to call her back when you're in a better mood, ok? We've had a long night, and don't need this aggravation."

She turned the compact towards Nathan, who without missing a beat said, "Yeah. Call back when you're done being mean to our friend. Oh yeah, whoever heard of a grouch who called herself 'Ms. Love?' That's just crazy." With that, Zora closed the compact with a loud 'CLACK.'

In the silence at the end of the call, the only sound was the squeaky chain of the nearby swings. The moment passed, and Daisy grabbed both them in for a huge hug. Nathan returned it happily and Zora suffered through without complaint. "You guys are the best," she said, wiping her eyes on her sleeve, " and I think you're right, Zora. No more secrets. I've got someone I want you to meet." Daisy put her hat back on and straightened her coat. "I think it's time we all heard what she has to say."

NATE SPARKS
THE BODYGUARD

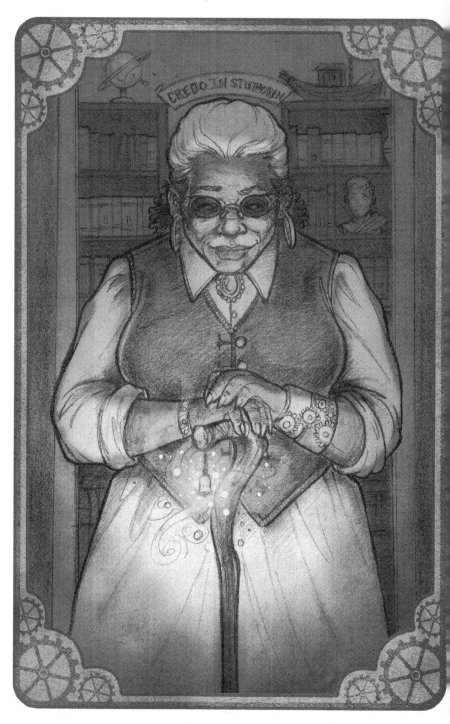

THE OLD WATCHER

Daisy landed in a part of Portland that the children didn't know, just as the bluish hue of night began to darken between the street lights. The neighborhood was nice, really nice in fact. There were large, old-styled homes lining the sidewalk, each with nicely trimmed yards and porches like Zora had seen in movies where grandparents would sit out on warm nights and chat about the weather. No matter how idyllic it appeared, Zora couldn't shake the feeling that something didn't quite fit there. It wasn't a bad feeling, more like a flipping sensation in the pit of her stomach. It felt like something was about to happen – the climb before the drop on a rollercoaster.

"Where are we, Daisy?" she asked as her feet touched down. "We're nowhere near our house."

"I just hope this isn't another birthday surprise," Nathan said with a nervous laugh, "because I think I'm all birthdayed-out. Yep, just ready for some cake and an early bedtime." He twisted the new bracelets on his wrists, quickly glancing at each shadowed driveway as they walked along at a brisk pace.

"We're safe, trust me." Daisy said. "I grew up on this street. There are safeguards here against danger." Just in case, Daisy reached into her hat and pulled out her charred umbrella. *Nothing wrong with being prepared,* she thought.

"Trust you? Seriously. We're supposed to just trust you?" Zora stopped immediately on the sidewalk, pulling Nate to halt as well. "Did you forget that we were just attacked by some kind of weird, masked ninjas with creepy weapons, and a heck of a lot of information on all of us – including you. Now you seem like you're afraid to take us home, or back to your super secret organization for help. Did I miss something?"

"Ok, ok! I don't know what I'm doing!" Daisy was tired and didn't realize she had yelled until she saw the surprised look on Nathan's face, then she instantly regretted it. Collecting herself, she tried again. "Look, guys, you don't have a lot of reason to follow me right now. I've been secretive, I know, but I'm really trying my best here. Another block and there'll be a house where we can rest, and maybe get some answers to your questions. Can you trust me that far?"

Zora had a stubborn look on her face, but before she could speak, Nathan grabbed Daisy's hand. "That's good enough for me," he said. "Lead on!"

Zora didn't argue.

The house they stopped at was surrounded by a white picket fence and the front yard was filled to overflowing with tall grass and wildflowers. The porch as well was covered in hanging baskets brimming with yellow, blue, and red blossoms and verdant green vines hanging over the railings. The shades were drawn, but a warm light could be seen inside the windows, and the murmur of conversation wafted outside and hung in the honeysuckle scented air. Atop the roof was a most peculiar weather vane that looked like some kind of goblin holding an elaborate spear covered in colored glass lenses.

Daisy stepped up on the porch, removed her hat, and straightened her coat. "I want you two to be on your best behavior. This is my family, so no back talk or smart remarks." She looked pointedly at Zora. "Try not to touch anything, and most importantly, don't stare."

"That doesn't sound very good," Zora replied.

"Don't worry so much. They're the nicest people you'll ever meet."

As she spoke, the floor dropped out, and the three of them fell into darkness.

They landed in a cube-shaped room that was lit only by small bursts of light, like distant stars in the soft, churning space that surrounded them. It was like floating in a piece of grape bubblegum.

"STATE YOUR BUSINESS, TRESPASSERS." A booming voice echoed through the void.

"Mr. Porter! It's me, Daisy!"

"WHO ARE YOU CALLING CRAZY, YOU GINGER SNAPDRAGON!" the voice boomed again. "I ASSURE YOU I AM SOUND OF MIND."

"No, not crazy – DAISY! It's Daisy Kidd, Mr. Porter."

"Let us out of here, you demented freak!" Zora yelled as she drifted in uncontrolled circles. When she looked around for her brother she saw Nathan bounce playfully off the walls and skillfully turning somersaults. "Nate! Stop that right now!"

"Why? It's like we're in the world's best bouncy house," he said, rocketing past Daisy, who grabbed him by the ankle. Slowly the room transformed into a more hospitable space, with leather armchairs and an old Persian rug, on which the three of them landed with a thud. Standing in front of them was a thin man with graying hair at his temples, nut brown skin, and a well-trimmed beard and mustache. He wore a crisp white shirt and striped tie, and over it all a flower print apron with the words "kiss the cook" stitched across the front. He adjusted his wire-framed glasses on his nose, and the hearing aid attached to it, before reaching to help them.

"Thanks, Lou. Kids, this is Mr. Porter. He used to be my boss." Daisy said.

"Sorry for the rude welcome, Little Flower," he said and kissed Daisy's hand. "Forgot to put in my device." He pointed to his ear. "Can't hear a thing without it, not to mention it's almost suppertime and you know we aren't used to late guests. I assume you're here to see your aunt." He gave the children a measuring glance. "So who are these two vagabonds? Up to mischief, I wager."

Nathan stepped forward, "I'm Nate Sparks, and this is my sister, Zora. Don't mind the scowl on her face, we were just almost killed by ninjas."

Mr. Porter's mustache twitched. "Ninjas, huh? Well, I expect you'll be staying for dinner then." Without another word, he turned and waved them up a flight of stairs, "Welcome to The Rookery. Mind your step."

<hr />

Inside of the house was a bustle of movement. Groups of elderly men and women sat in animated conversation while others were in the middle of magical feats. By the looks on their faces, Daisy could tell that Zora and Nathan were very impressed. Two men sat arguing in a corner over a machine that had obviously malfunctioned since both of them kept transforming back and forth into chickens. Across the hall there appeared to be a rousing game of mid-air checkers – although this version seemed to be full contact. Amidst all of the amazing sights, something dawned on Zora.

"Is this an old folk's home?" she said quietly to Daisy, but not quietly enough.

"Who you callin' old, Ms. Sparks?" Mr. Porter blustered through his thick mustache. "This is a home for retired explorers, adventurers, mages, and makers. These are some of the greatest minds of a generation." Nearby in the kitchen there was a large explosion, followed by a cloud of flour and smoke as a number of people fell through the doorway calling out, "Rolls are done!" each waving at Daisy like old friends as she and the children walked by. Mr. Porter shook his head and mumbled, "Well, they were the greatest minds of a generation."

A large, red disc came zipping in from the other room, barely missing Daisy's head. It ricocheted off an oak column, smashed through an expensive looking lamp and came barreling towards Zora.

"Look out!" Nate yelled. He tapped his bracelets together, and in flash, he grabbed onto the disk with his gleaming gauntlets and was lifted high into the air. He wrestled with the disk as it twisted and turned in his grasp, spinning him this way and that. The ceiling was high, which gave him plenty of space to shoot back and forth, legs flailing about.

"That's enough, thank you," said a commanding voice, followed by the clear sound of a bell ringing. The disk wavered for a moment, then fell along with Nathan six feet onto an old sofa Mr. Porter had quickly pushed under him. It took Nathan a second to collect himself, but when he did, a stout black woman with dark glasses and a gray bowler hat was standing over him holding a gnarled cane above her head. "Are you alright young man?" she said in that same commanding voice as before, though softened with concern.

"Yes ma'am," he replied. He stood up quickly and extended his hand, which was still covered in the large gauntlet. "Thanks for the save."

She patted him on the head. "Don't mention it. These games of checkers can get a little unruly close to dinnertime."

Daisy came running, catching the woman up in a big hug. "Aunt Mizzy! Kids, this is the illustrious Mildred Mizner, but I call her Aunt Mizzy." She was talking super fast, and couldn't seem to stop grinning. "She used to be the head of the Laurel Society, where I work – but she retired a few years ago after almost fifty years. Incredible right? Say hi!"

Ms. Mizner smiled warmly. "Hello, sweetie. I had a feeling that you'd be coming around tonight, and with guests I noticed."

"Of course you did!"

Zora stood and tilted her head slightly. "Hi," she said, with a fair amount of skepticism in her voice. "So you were the head of this society since, what, the 1950s? These Laurel guys sound pretty progressive."

Ms. Mizner positioned her cane before her and tilted her head slightly as well. "Not as much as one might hope," she replied with a smile, "but like most powerful black woman, I was progressive enough to change their minds."

"Oh, I'm going to like her," Nate said.

Daisy gave her young charge a withering look. "How's about a little more respect, you two. Mizzy is a very important person around here," she said before turning back to her aunt. "You won't believe what happened to us!" Before she could get into the story, Ms. Mizner raised her a finger to her lips and shook her head.

"Let's move this conversation into the den, shall we?" she said and walked off down the hall. "Thank you for your help, Louis."

Mr. Porter gave a short bow to them all. "My pleasure, Mizzy. I'll be sure to set some extra plates for dinner as well. Hope you're all hungry." With that, he hurried off towards the kitchen.

Ms. Mizner led Daisy and the children down the hall to a set of large double doors, above which were the words CREDO IN STUPOREM deeply carved into the lintel and inlaid with gold leaf. Inside was a comfortable room, with deep armchairs, stacks of books, and the welcoming smell of cinnamon. The middle of the hardwood floor bore a circular crest – a bowler hat surrounded with laurel leaves with a question mark dead center. The rest of the room could have doubled as an oddities thrift shop – every surface was filled with old photos, strange contraptions, ancient tapestries, and statuary from far off places. Once they were inside, Ms. Mizner closed the door and tapped it with the head of her cane. It gave off the same ring as before, and instantly the entryway faded away, leaving only another wall covered in photographs.

"Auntie, these are my charges," Daisy said excitedly, "this is…"

"Oh hush child. I know these kiddos." Ms. Misner stepped forward and adjusted her dark, almost black, spectacles. "Welcome to our home. I want you to know that you're safe here."

Zora stood with her arms crossed. "This is your aunt?" Daisy bobbed her redhead in a cheery sort of way, but when Zora looked back at the short, grey-headed black woman, she couldn't help but say, "You two don't look like family."

To this, Mildred Mizner let out the loudest laugh Zora had ever heard from an old lady. It was long, and deep, and punctuated occasionally with snorts and little giggles. Mildred pulled her glasses down to the end of her nose, showing them the milky whites of her almost sightless eyes. "Yes, she's my girl. I took her on when she just a babe. As far as looking like family, truly darlin' I never really noticed."

Zora felt her face go flush and she looked away. "Sorry, ma'am," she mumbled, but mostly to her shoes. "I didn't know you were blind."

"Well baby, there are a lot of ways to see, so don't you worry. You're direct, Ms. Sparks. I like a little directness. I was the head of Portland Laurel Society for over forty years, and I learned to appreciate people who can get straight to the point. So, let me get a better measure of you two." She looked the young Mr. Sparks up and down, rubbing her chin between her thumb and forefinger. "You must be Nathan. Middle name, Elias. Peculiar. Impetuous sort, with a love of kung fu films, books about samurai, and rocky road ice cream. Happy birthday, by the way." Nathan stood stunned. Ms. Mizner turned to Zora again. "And you, Ms. Sparks – bright, adventurous, bold when it comes to invention, but cautious with new people and your personal affairs. I've been waiting a long time to meet you."

"How is that? We don't know you, and even Daisy didn't know we were coming here." Zora looked at her questioningly. "Or did she?"

"Of course not," Daisy said, annoyed at the implications. "You see kids, Aunt Mizzy is what we in the Society call a Watcher – a magic practitioner who has the rare ability to see the world without time."

"Without time? Does that mean you can see into the past, or into the future?" Zora said. There was something in her voice, a kind of suppressed excitement. Daisy noticed it right away.

"Let's just say it's a little of both," Ms. Mizner replied. "What I see are connections between what is, what was, and what could be. It's not an exact science," she said, leaning towards them, "but frankly, I'm better at it than most."

"So you knew about whoever attacked us tonight?" Zora asked.

"I know a great many things, Zora my dear. Things that it is well past time that I shared, but let's discuss them in more suitable surroundings," Ms. Mizner said.

"Isn't that why you closed that crazy door," Nathan said, pointing at what was now a wall.

"Oh heavens no." Ms. Mizner walked to the edge of the crest on the floor and tapped it three times with her cane. Three long rings sounded out, the last of which ringing far longer than it should, and slowly the crest split and dropped away, opening into a deep passageway. They all looked over the edge and watched as steps began to appear, leading down into the dark well. When the grinding sound of sliding stones ended, Zora, Nathan, and Daisy felt a damp, chilling wind blow up from the opening. "Follow me, children," Ms. Mizner said smiling. "There's little light, so be careful. It only gets trickier from here."

MILDRED MIZNER
THE ORACLE

SECRETS OF
THE LAUREL SOCIETY

The entrance closed quickly behind Daisy and the children, but they continued down even as the way before them disappeared into the darkness. The air grew cooler with each step, carrying a light smell of moisture coming off of the cold stones. There wasn't a railing to speak of so they kept close to the wall, which was covered with deeply carved lines and grooves that followed the curve of the peculiar stair.

"All this magic about, and nobody has a flashlight," Zora groaned then stumbled. Nathan caught her arm and pulled her back from the edge of the step, trying his best not to look down into the chasm below.

"I've got something," Daisy reached into her bowler and rummaged around. "That's not it," she murmured, all the way up to her shoulder in the hat, "Oh, that's not it either. Is that what I think it is? I could have sworn I lost this."

"Allow me, sweety," Ms. Mizner said, and with another ring of her cane, a dozen shimmering blue lights appeared. They hung in the air around the handle of her cane like fireworks suspended in space, but it was what they revealed that was so breathtaking. What they had thought were mere designs on the wall were actually images. Surrounding them in the well were hieroglyphs and ancient stories carved in relief, some with figures in robes teaching and studying, while others were of the same figures wielding staffs or producing power from their very fingers in some huge battle.

The light fell on many scenes. Zora paused to examine the wall, trying to take them all in. "These carvings must be thousands of years old," she said. "I see Egyptian motifs, as well as Nubian and Olmec. That over there looks like Sumerian," she said. "Where did they all come from?"

"Far off and mysterious places," Ms. Mizner replied, "and it took a great deal of time to transport them here. I remember the first time I saw the Well of Memory. I was only a little older than you, and of course, I could actually see back then."

As Aunt Mizzy and Zora talked, Daisy could feel her face flush with annoyance. The whole idea that there was yet another secret to the Laurel Society, especially one her aunt had never revealed, was getting Daisy angrier by the second. "So now she's an expert in ancient carvings?" Daisy whispered to Nathan, trying her best to sound unfazed. "When did that happen exactly?"

"I don't know," he whispered back, "she's a geek who reads too much. That's what they do."

At that moment, Daisy stopped in midstep on the stair, her attention drawn to a broad scene along the wall. In it, the robed figures stood with their hands raised against something – smaller figures who seemed to give off an aura of power that was brought to life in the wavering glow of her aunt's summoned light. "Why haven't you ever brought me down here, Aunt Mizzy?" Daisy asked, pulling her attention away from the relief. "I mean, I've brought you tea in that den since I was five years old, and never once did you think to tell me that there was a hidden…whatever this is. I have to admit, this is kind of annoying."

"It wasn't your time to see it, Daisy. You're just going to have to trust me on that," Ms. Mizner said, never missing a step as she continued her descent.

When they reached the bottom, the well opened up into a large antechamber. At the far end was a tall door, bound with silver latches. Ms. Mizner came to it and placed the head of her cane on a symbol engraved on the door handle, and the doors opened.

"Come in everyone," she said, waving them inside.

This room could only be compared to a museum. Tall, cathedral-like walls surrounded the circular space, and set back in alcoves along the wall were artifacts and oddities that were not to be believed. There were shelves upon shelves covered with leather bound tomes, stacks of parchment scrolls, and statuary made from black onyx, bronze, and even gold. Medieval flying machines hung from the dome ceiling, which was covered with an enormous fresco painting of swirling stars. On closer examination, one would notice that the stars were in constant motion like a twisting nebula of blue and red sparks winking in and out of existence. Flanking the ceiling were tall stone faces carved into the wall, each keeping silent watch over the treasures below. At the very center of the chamber was a circular pool. Its sides were tiled with gold, turquoise, and silver, and in its center stood a raised dais, on top of which sat a tarnished copper astrolabe fitted with colored lenses, covered in strange markings, and radiating a warm cascade of light.

"Zora, I hate to tell you this," Nate said, "but I think she's got your secret sanctum beat – and hard."

"That's not very nice, Nathan," Daisy said, but even as a practitioner of the Wonderous Science, Daisy had to admit this room was one of the most magnificent places she had ever seen. The level of history here was beyond anything she had ever read in the magical history books.

"As I'm sure you and your sister have many of your own treasures, I will take that as a true compliment, Mr. Sparks," Ms. Mizner said. She took a seat at the edge of the pool and stretched. "It was 1849 when all of this was moved to Portland over the course of a hundred years, each item found in remote corners of the world and brought here for safe keeping. Even the Laurel Society doesn't know this room exists, and it's been my responsibility to keep this observatory the most guarded of magical secrets."

"Observatory?" Zora said, "We're underground. What could we possibly be observing?"

"Let me show you." Ms. Mizner reached her hand into the pool, swirling her finger in slow circles and humming quietly to herself. It was a pleasant tune, one that reminded Daisy of the restless nights when her aunt would sing her to sleep. When Mizzy pulled her hand from the water, it had taken on a glow – an aura like the hazy twinkle of distant Christmas lights danced around her fingertips. "This is etherea – the most abundant element of magic. It is drawn to creativity and the imaginative mind, and makes the Wonderous Science possible."

Zora moved closer, in cautious awe of what she was seeing. "I knew it," she whispered. "I've always known there was something that made it all work, but I...I never knew it was so beautiful." She reached out her hand, touching her fingertips to Ms. Mizner's, and felt the warmth wash over her. "I've never seen anything like this. How are you doing it?"

Just then, a voice spoke up from the back of the chamber. "The process is quite intriguing," it said, and they all turned sharply to see a large figure shift near one of the book shelves. What they had originally thought was a large statue was walking towards them, rumbling the ground with each advancing step. As it moved they heard stones grinding against one another.

"ZORA!!" Nathan jumped in front of his sister, bringing up his Dynamo Fists ready for an attack. "Rock monster… it's a rock monster!"

It stepped into the light of the fountain. Standing before them was indeed a man made of stone, almost eight feet tall with wide, armored shoulders, large hands, and piercing gray eyes. He wore a long, blue tunic over his hulking frame that trailed down to his bare feet. Even Daisy stood frozen in amazement for a moment until she noticed a slight smile play across her aunt's face.

"Hello, Mildred. I see you brought guests," the stone man said politely. His voice was strangely pleasant despite its heavy tone, like an echo in a deep cavern.

"Calm down you three." Ms. Mizner rose and patted the stone man on his giant arm. "I'd like to you to meet Orin. He's a dear friend of mine." She waited for a moment, but there was no response from the kids. "Well, did you all forget your manners?"

With a prod from Daisy, the Sparks managed to stammer out a "hello" in unison.

"Greetings all," he said with a bow, "I didn't mean to scare you, young ones."

"Scare us! I almost needed new shorts!" Nathan said and deactivated his fists. "What were you doing sneaking up on us like that? Not cool, rock dude. Not cool. What are you anyway?"

Orin stood to his full, imposing height and raised his fist in some kind of salute. "I am the last of the Shona Warriors, protector of the ancient Ugod u Chadra," he relaxed a bit after that, looking a little embarrassed, "…or, at least I use to be. The Stone Lords are all gone now, and I haven't been a warrior in a very long time. I protect the observatory now, and these books and artifacts are my life."

Now that the initial shock had faded a bit, Zora noticed the large book in his hand. "Is that *Abner's History of Obscure Concepts in Theoretical Engineering?*" Zora said, barely containing herself, and a curious smile came to Orin's broad face. "I've always wanted to read it, but I didn't think there were copies still around."

"Why yes it is, and an original printing. Fascinating, isn't it?" Orin held the book for Zora to see. "The diagrams are incredible. Thomas Abner was quite the practitioner in the early 1700s, until that whole 'witch burning' problem. I was reading a few passages when you arrived. I get so engrossed sometimes that I don't notice Mildred when she comes by. She has to wake me from my daydreaming," he chuckled. "She has a very light step, you know."

Ms. Mizner introduced them all, and each received a bow. "So this is your Daisy?" Orin smiled. "You're as beautiful as your aunt described."

"Thanks," Daisy said, feeling a bit awkward getting compliments from a giant stone man. Even having known about the Wonderous Science her entire life, she never could have imagined having a conversation with anyone as amazing as Orin. "You were saying? About the fountain, I mean."

Ms. Mizner raised her hand before Orin could speak. "There are more pressing matters, I'm afraid," she said. "These young people have just escaped terrible danger, and we need to address the trouble at hand." There was concern in her voice, and a deep furrow in her brow. "Their attackers called themselves The Blades of The Balance."

Orin's cheerful expression faded instantly. "The Balance? Here? Now?" He turned and headed for the shelves, anxiously pulling books from the collected volumes in a desperate search for something. "No, no, no. It's too soon. He said he'd keep it safe. He said it was hidden."

"I don't get it, what's he talking about?" Zora said as they all rushed to keep up with Orin's huge stride, all except Ms. Mizner who sauntered along behind them.

"Beats me," Daisy shouted, running alongside her. "Until today I didn't even know any of this existed. That's the problem with SECRET societies!"

When they caught up with him, Orin had pulled a large tome from the shelf and was quickly leafing through the pages. Mildred walked up to her friend and placed her hand on his. "You're in a tizzy, I know," she said in a gentle tone, "but maybe you should let these young people know what's going on. Sound good?"

Orin looked up at them, remembering he wasn't alone in the observatory. "Yes, of course. My apologies," he said and straightened his tunic, regaining his composure. "You must all understand, this is unprecedented. The Balance acting in the open, attacking a member of the

Society with two of her charges, it's unheard of. This group has always operated in the shadows, hiding within the community of practitioners like ghosts. They have long been thought to have disappeared, but there were always whispered rumors of their presence, just beyond the notice of those in power."

"You might want to go into a *little* more detail," Daisy said, noticing the confused looks on Zora and Nathan's faces. "Start at the beginning."

Orin began again. "The concept of magic, you see, has not always been as it is today. There was a time, centuries ago, when this power flowed as easily through our world as water in a river. It came from beyond and was manifested in the form of etherea. Etherea is one of the miraculous elements of creation, and is the basis of all acts of magic, allowing beings to bend and shape the very laws of reality to their need and purpose. It suffused everything with its power, and accessing it was merely a matter of will and study." He turned the pages of the book to an illustration of a disturbing scene. In it, men and women from every corner of the world were engaged in some kind of battle with magic as their weapons. "However, like any great resource," he continued, "etherea was sought after by the malign as well as the virtuous. Societies formed amongst practitioners that competed for the secrets of magic, vying with each other for power. A war seemed imminent, one the likes of which had never been seen and would devastate all life in our world." He turned the pages again, this time stopping at an image of five robed figures standing together, each with a ball of light suspended in their outstretched hand. There were four men and one woman, each as different from each other as they could be. One even seemed to have some kind of flaming head! "In the early fourth century, a small group of legendary practitioners convened with hopes of stopping the conflict before it destroyed everything," Orin said with a sense of reverence. "Today we call them the Great Masters: Miliyons the Wanderer, Nofret the Scribe, Wei Xan the Wise, Nicholas the Maker, and Arcon the Blade. They were faced with a desperate situation that forced them to make a desperate decision. To forestall a war, they crafted an artifact together that diminished the flow of all etherea to our world to a mere fraction of its true strength."

"So to stop a few people from misusing magic, they lessened it for everybody else?" Zora said. "That seems a little drastic."

"As I said, it was a desperate time," Orin replied, "and they didn't stop magic, exactly. Think of it more like damming a river, restricting the flow for those who could access magic. By doing this, they hoped to limit those who had the knowledge and skill to use etherea, and keep it out of the hands of those they considered dangerous. And so the Wonderous Science was established – a system of order built into the very fabric of magic."

Zora rolled her eyes, obviously less than convinced. "Still seems like overkill to me. They essentially buttered their bread with a broadsword."

Nathan stifled a laugh. "Broadsword," he snorted. "Classic."

"You are not the first to question their actions," Orin said, replacing the book on its shelf. "A clandestine group of mages formed a secret brotherhood, seeding agents into every society they could across the world, seeking to return magic to its original state where etherea flowed unfettered. They called themselves The Balance."

"Like the masked men we met tonight," Daisy said. She felt a cold chill go through her as she remembered their eyes blazing in the darkness and the hissing crackle of their weapons.

"I'm afraid so. They knew the only way to achieve their goal was to locate the whereabouts of the artifact created by the Great Masters, but it has been lost for almost fifteen hundred years. They were determined, and though their numbers were small, they worked with deadly efficiency. Some thought they were freedom fighters or revolutionaries, but their methods proved to be too brutal. Soon, every society hunted them down and weeded out their agents. They haven't been heard from for close to a century – not until today."

"The last they were seen was in 1929, in a small village in East Africa," Ms. Mizner said as she walked over to a large cushioned chair and sat down. "A man by the name of Elias Rathmore, who was an industrialist from here in Portland, had traveled the globe looking for lost treasures related to the Wonderous Science. He was a powerful practitioner but wasn't a member of a society – he enjoyed his freedom too much. He had followed a lifetime's worth of clues and braved many dangers and found his way to a ruin outside of Khartoum on the southern border of Egypt. There he made a discovery that would change the course of his life, and the fate of the world."

"Was it the artifact?" Zora asked.

"Yes. He was pursued by others to the ruin. They were called the Thule Society, and they wanted desperately to take Rathmore's discovery back to their home in Germany. Unknown to the Thule, agents of The Balance were in their ranks as well, but before they could get their hands on their prize, Rathmore made a brash move." She paused for effect and seemed to enjoy the palpable anticipation that hung in the air around her before she spoke again. "Rather than have it fall into these villains hands, he destroyed the artifact."

"Oh come on!" Nate blurted out, drawing surprised stares from Daisy, Zora, and even Orin. "You're telling me that this guy tomb raided his way across the planet only to blow up what he was looking for? BOOOO!"

"I would have done the same thing," Zora said confidently and punched her brother in the shoulder. "He knew they were going to do something bad with it. Better to destroy it than chance them getting their sticky hands on it."

"Zora considers herself an expert on E.W. Rathmore," Daisy said, "we even went to his exhibit. It was an…interesting experience." She glanced at the children and noticed them tense.

"Rathmore's choice was brought on by fear," Ms. Mizner said in a grave voice. "He was a man who traveled the world alone, trusting no one with his secrets or to aid him, and when his time came to make this choice there was no one there for him to trust for help." She stood and started back towards the door of the observatory, but stopped as she reached the fountain. "Do you know what the consequence of that decision was?" No one answered. "He left the world to a decade without magic. Practitioners call this period The 7th Waning, but you know it better as The Great Depression."

Zora and Nathan were speechless.

"He caused The Great Depression," Zora eventually said, "with one bad decision?"

"Yes. One he spent the rest of his life trying to rectify." Ms. Mizner said. "I can only hope, if I had a tough choice like that to make, that I had someone I trusted there to help me through it." She continued on towards the door, gesturing them to follow.

"That's it, Aunt Mizzy?" Daisy asked. "You brought us down here to the extra-special-secret chamber, filled with artifacts and a giant stone man, and we aren't even going to talk about what happened at Amazo's?"

"Sweety, I'm an old woman, and we've discussed quite enough for one night. We're all tired, and it's dinnertime, so I insist you all stay the night. You'll be safe, and I'll let the Society know you're here." Ms. Mizner then turned to Orin. "See you tomorrow, my friend. We need to finish our bridge game from earlier."

"I'm looking forward to it," he replied, bowing deeply. "It was a great pleasure to meet you all. Safe travels."

Zora was just about to follow along with Ms. Mizner, Daisy, and Nathan, but just before she left, she stopped near the door and turned. "I hope I can come back and see you again, Orin," she said, "and maybe I can bring a friend I think you would really like to meet."

Orin's stoney face lit up with a bright smile. "I would like that very much," he replied.

‹‹‹›››

Dinner at The Rookery was a madhouse, but in the best possible way. Zora, Nathan, and Daisy spent the rest of the night scooping heaping spoonfuls of pot roast and potatoes, spinach casserole, and hot yams from steaming trays that marched around the dining room table on spindly copper legs. Ms. Mizner sat at the head of the table serenely smiling as the rest of the house's occupants carried on conversations amidst the sounds of raucous laughter and the clinking of glasses and utensils on plates. Everyone there had a story to tell about Daisy when she was a little girl, and before the meal was done she was blushing as red as her hair.

Mr. Porter had beds made up for them in the spare room upstairs, and they were allowed to take their desert with them. Over plates of pecan pie, Daisy told Zora and Nathan some of her less embarrassing memories of living in that strange and wonderful house.

"Mom would love it here," Zora whispered to Daisy as she lay looking out the window into the starry night. It was the last thing she said before drifting off. Soon, each of them was fast asleep.

ORIN
THE LIBRARIAN

THE TROUBLE WITH SECRETS

Daisy woke the next morning feeling rested, but strangely unsettled down to her core. She stared at the ceiling of their room, watching as the dawn light crept slowly across the striped wallpaper. By the time it was six o'clock, she had been rolling worries around in her head for close to an hour. Daisy could barely stand it. There had been just too many coincidences going on in Zora and Nathan's lives to be ignored, and she was embarrassed that she could not see the connections. She was so focused on impressing them and doing a good job that she had missed something, and now they were in real danger.

The truth of the matter was, no matter how much she wanted to ignore it, Zora was far from the normal charge with potential powers, and her Adept level of power could make her dangerous. It was Daisy's responsibility to get to the bottom of whatever danger they were in before Zora did something drastic. At that moment, she glanced over at the two beds across the room and noticed one was empty. Zora was gone, taking her shoes, satchel, and the terry cloth robe Mr. Porter had left at the foot of her bed.

"I'm pretty sure that girl is a ninja," Daisy mumbled. Across the room, Nathan snored in agreement.

Zora slipped down the stairs, heading to the kitchen. When she walked into the room, she was only a little surprised to see Mildred Mizner sitting at a small table by the window with a large, steaming mug in her hand. She was exactly the person Zora had wanted to find, and somehow, Ms. Mizner seemed to have been waiting.

"Hey early riser," she said, quietly sipping.

"I wasn't sneaking out," Zora said quickly.

"I thought nothing of the sort," she replied and patted the chair beside her. "Come have some tea and toast with me. Nothing beats tea and toast when there are things on your mind."

Zora sat down while Ms. Mizner poured her a cup and slid a plate heaped with brown toast covered in butter and dark jam in front of her. "Blackberry was always my favorite," she chuckled, "back when I was just a little thing like you I couldn't get enough of it."

Zora took a bite of the toast and sipped at the tea, which was strong and smelled like mint and flowers. They were both very good and they did make her feel a little bit better. "You knew I was going to come down here, didn't you?" she asked. "Did you see it with your powers?"

"Not really," Mildred replied. "I've always been an early bird too. Just figured we might have that in common. Not to mention, I'm sure you have a lot of questions. Figured we'd just jump right in. Was I wrong?"

"No, ma'am," Zora replied. She looked out through the window at the tall wildflowers surrounding the house, still glistening with morning dew. The blooms should have been gone this late in the season, but there they were, defying expectations. "My mother used to sit up in the morning with me, just like this," she said, "and we wouldn't really talk all that much, but she always seemed to know just when to say something. Like she was reading my mind."

"Good moms have that ability," Ms. Mizner said, taking a sip of her tea. "We can always tell when our kiddos need us, even if all they need is for us to sit and listen. Daisy used to wake up early like this, too. She was never much one for tea, but she could put toast and jam away like it was going out of style. That girl was a bottomless pit when she was your age."

Zora couldn't help but smile at the thought of a miniature Daisy Kidd making her way through piles of toast. The image sustained her through the long silence and quiet sipping of tea. She wanted to talk to Ms. Mizner, to tell her what was going on, but it was always so hard to know when to share this kind of stuff. Before long, she slowly pulled the red journal from her satchel. She took the chain from around her neck and placed the Master Gear on top of the book and slid them across the table until they touched Ms. Mizner's resting hand. "This is what those guys were after last night. My mom gave them to me before she had to go away to the hospital. It's one of E.W. Rathmore's journals. She told me to take care of them, and that they were important. I'm sure Daisy already told you, but I wanted you to hear it from me."

Instead of reaching for the artifact, Mildred took Zora's hand and gave it a gentle squeeze. Although her hands were thin with age, there was something about them – a comforting strength that defied her years.

"Don't worry about that, sweetie," she said. "Daisy kept your secrets safe. She's isn't someone that takes a promise lightly. As for the this," she motioned towards the gear, "I knew about the artifact before she ever met you. It was why I sent her there in the first place. I've been waiting for it to come into your possession for quite a long time. Nearly eighty-five years in fact."

"Eighty-five years! You've known about me since 1921?" Zora said, trying her best to not sound so skeptical. "I'm guessing that's your future-vision again? Must be pretty handy."

"It can be, but it's not as precise as you seem to think. The vision I had of you, however, was quite clear." Mildred removed her glasses. "I should know since it was the last thing I ever saw with these old eyes."

Hearing that took the wind out of Zora all at once. There was no possible way to properly respond to a revelation like that, and she found herself fumbling for words. "A vision of me was the last thing you saw? You say that like it … b-blinded you?" she stuttered. It was strange, she had only just met this woman the night before, but there was something about her – a familiarity or connection. She sat up and wrapped her arms around her in a tight embrace. "I'm so sorry," she whispered, fighting back unexpected tears. Mildred hugged her back just as tightly.

"Oh, child," she said, her voice deep and soothing, "it's a sacrifice I'd make again to see your sweet face." When Zora let go, Mildred gently cupped her hands around the young girl's face. "You are going to have a tough road ahead, you hear. My vision doesn't go beyond this moment, and even now your future is beginning to take shape in ways I can't predict. To be totally honest," she tapped her finger on the red journal, "I didn't even know you had Rathmore's journal, and with powers like mine, being surprised is a novelty."

"My mother said that there were secrets in the journal – powerful secrets," Zora said. "She warned me not to read it, and above all to keep the gear hidden. I thought that maybe I could use them, you know. I thought that I could use it to make everything better."

"Magic is a strange thing, Zora. Everything it touches changes, and suddenly nothing is the same. This book is an artifact of the Wonderous Science – of magic – and has been lost as long as the Master Gear. I believe that it will be very important in events to come. I can't say with certainty, but I fear you will face great challenges very soon. Even now, things are starting to change." She slid the book and the Master Gear back to Zora. "I can't see what awaits you on your path, but I do know that you were meant to have these."

"You sure about that?" Zora said, looking down at her cup. "I haven't done much good with them so far."

"Zora Sparks, there is greatness in you, I know it, but you have a lot to learn. First and foremost is that you can't make it through this life alone. You are gonna have to trust your family and friends to stand with you. None of us can make it on our own. Trust me."

"That sounds like something Daisy said."

Ms. Mizner winked. "Where do you think she heard it from?"

"At first I thought Daisy was kind of corny," Zora said, "but I sort of get it now. You know, Ms. Mizner, she's really lucky to have an aunt like you."

"Oh sweetie, after all of this, I think you should call me Aunt Mizzy." She poured Zora another cup of tea. "Let's sit a while longer, shall we? Daisy and Nathan, you're welcome to join us."

Zora turned to see her brother and Daisy crouched near the door to the kitchen. "How long have you been listening?" she asked.

"Just long enough," Daisy replied with a smile.

Daisy, Zora and Nate had spent the early hours of the day at the Rookery trying to leave, which was difficult since their new friends were reluctant to see them go. The retirees kept wanting to share ideas and demonstrate old wonderous items for Zora and Nathan's delight. After lunch, and a few goodbyes, Daisy prepared to fly her charges home.

"I'm sure Mr. Flint and Stephanie will be expecting a report today," Ms. Mizner said before they left. "Get the children home and let their aunt know they are ok first. You've all had an interesting night, and I'm sure you could use a little rest before you head into that storm at the Chapter House."

"You think it'll be safe," Daisy asked, "taking them home, I mean?"

"I'll call ahead for you so the Society can have some Daggers meet you there. We'll make sure things are taken care of."

They hugged, Daisy breathing deep of her aunt's familiar scent – lavender and with the slightest hint of peppermint. "I love you, Mizzy," she said.

"And I love you, Daisy dear. Be careful."

⁓

On the way back, Daisy felt like she was really getting the hang of her flying, and since Teresa wasn't due back until the next day, they didn't rush getting back to 1515 Anders Place. Instead, she and the children stopped by Salt & Straw to get ice cream first and took the scenic route through the park. She kept her compact deep in her pocket – not wanting to face the music from Stephanie and Mr. Flint just yet.

By the time they made it home it was late afternoon, but even as they landed a block from the house, Zora and Nate could tell something wasn't quite right. Standing on their porch were two men in dark suits and red waistcoats, both wearing white gloves and dark expressions on their faces.

"Who are they?" Nate said, rubbing his wrists. "Please tell me it's not those Blade guys again."

Daisy knew right away who they were. "Those are Daggers. They're society members, like me," she said.

"Blades, Daggers – either way, they sound sharp and dangerous. Bad news all around." Nate said.

"Any idea what they're doing here?" Zora asked.

Daisy hesitated. "They're here for our protection, I guess. Although, they do look kind of cross, don't they?" She straightened her coat and her bowler almost instinctually. "Come on. What's the worse that could happen?"

Nathan grimaced. "Never say that!" he hissed. "Those are the famous last words of so many dummies in all those horror movies Teresa thinks I'm not watching when she goes to bed."

Zora took Daisy's hand, which was unexpected to say the lease, and thrust something into it. It was her red journal – the Rathmore journal. "Just in case the worse does happen, I probably shouldn't have both of these on me," she said, "I trust you to know what to do with this in the case of an emergency?"

"No! Not really." Daisy didn't really know how else to respond, but eventually nodded acceptance as they made their way up the walk to the porch.

One of the two Daggers greeted them and opened the door as if they were the strangers there. "Mr. Flint is waiting for you inside," he said, and Daisy heard herself audibly gulp. In the living room sat the oddest collection of people she had ever seen; Hobbs stood stoically beside Mr. Flint who sat comfortably on the floral sofa, slim and sharp as a tack, and sipping from a mug that read *Stay Calm and Drink Tea*. Sitting beside him were Johann (uncomfortably avoiding eye contact) and Marco, both holding large boxes of what appeared to be items from Zora's workshop. Across from them was Teresa, looking confused and more than a little anxious.

"Welcome Ms. Kidd," Mr. Flint said in his clipped accent. "We were expecting you back sooner, but seeing as the children are safe, we can move past your tardiness to more pressing matters."

Nate ran up to Teresa and gave her a big hug. "Hi Aunt T! I thought you weren't coming back until tomorrow," he said, sounding genuinely happy to see her.

"I was, but I got a call that you guys were in some kind of trouble," she replied and turned to Zora and

Daisy, "I tried to call you on the way home but it kept going to voice mail. Now Mr. Flint here is saying there was an accident at Amazo's. What happened?"

Mr. Flint leaned forward and carefully sat the mug on the coffee table. "Ms. Madison, in light of the events of last night at the arcade, and Ms. Kidd absconding with the children, I feel I must take the blame." He turned his flat gaze towards Daisy. "Ms. Kidd has been one of our least trustworthy employees for some time, but we took your case as an opportunity for her to prove herself to our agency. Her failure is our failure, and with the new information we have about Zora, we understand that pairing her with these children was a mistake."

"Hey! You take that back!" Nathan shouted.

Daisy felt like the wind had been knocked out of her, but even as her hopes and plans for the future seem to catch fire right before her eyes, she noticed the fear on Zora's face. "What 'new information' are you talking about?" she said, managing a calm she didn't know she had.

"Let's cut to the point, Ms Madison – Zora isn't like other children in the system. Her intelligence, defiant nature, and inventive abilities makes her a possible danger to herself and others. Our organization, as both caretakers and contracted agents of the state, is obliged to make observations when someone like her is in custody." As he spoke, Mr. Flint motioning to Johann and Marco. "Our investigators here have found some troubling items in Ms. Spark's private space – some of which could be considered dangerous weapons. Isn't that true gentlemen?"

Marco nodded, but Johann hesitated before speaking. "I guess some of this could be considered dangerous, but only under certain circumstances…"

Flint stopped him short. "Thank you, Mr. Epstein. That is quite enough."

Teresa's face went pale, and she turned to Zora. "What is he talking about, Zoe?"

For the first time since she had met her, Daisy saw Zora freeze in total fear.

"It's not what…I mean…I didn't…"

"No need to explain, Ms. Sparks," Flint said. "Ms. Madison, in light of the failure of our employee, Ms. Kidd, to bring these frightful items to your attention, her employment is hereby terminated." Daisy felt those words like a hard blow to her stomach, but Mr. Flint continued. "Furthermore, it is of my professional opinion, in light of her family history of mental illness, that Zora may very well be a danger to herself and others."

Hearing this, Teresa stood and positioned herself between him and the children. "Now wait just a minute," she said, a hint of growing anger in her voice. "I'm not sure I like you making assumptions about my niece like that. Sure, this is all getting a little out of hand, but…"

Once again, Mr. Flint stopped her short. "Ms. Madison, I've seen this play out many times before. When it comes to children with Zora's abilities, it's easy to miss the early warning signs, especially when they are in the care of young and untried parental figures. With the added needs of young Mr. Sparks, it is obvious they are too much for you to handle. Ms. Sparks' moods and temperament will only become worse, leading to disastrous ends. Luckily, my company has experience with troubled youths like her, and our facility is specially equipped to handle the special needs of these children. Shroudhurst Hospital is a fine establishment, and can provide her with the structure and help she needs."

"A hospital?" Teresa said. "Are you serious? What would make you think she needed to go some place like that?"

Mr. Flint cut his eyes towards Daisy. "It was Ms. Kidd's assignment to make this determination, but since she couldn't carry out her duties, it falls to me to make this right."

Daisy turned, and the look of horror that came over Zora's face made her insides go cold. She'd never seen her look so conflicted, hurt, and betrayed. She wanted to reach out to her, to tell her that it wasn't true. But it was – it was all true.

"You said you were here to help us," Zora said, her voice barely a whisper, "and I trusted you."

"I was – I mean, I am here to help you," Daisy said, feebly trying to find the words. "I would never let them take you away from here, you know that right?"

"Do I?" Zora replied.

I can't fail them. The thought came to Daisy, clear and sure as any she had ever had. *I won't fail them.* Daisy then turned to meet Mr. Flint's hard gaze. "Sir, you have the wrong idea about Zora," she said with a confidence that surprised even her. "You have the wrong idea about this whole family!" Daisy stepped forward and jabbed her finger against her boss's chest. From the corner of her eye, she noticed Hobbs step forward, cracking his knuckles, but at this point, she really didn't care. "You wouldn't believe the night we had – the dangers that we faced together. These kids are extraordinary! They face off against The Blades of the Balance and lived."

Teresa's eyes got really wide. "Excuse me?" she said, looking very confused at this point.

"I'll tell you later," Daisy replied, pushing on before she lost her nerve. "The point is they are special, Teresa too, and they all need each other. It doesn't matter what you think you see in their future. You don't know the great things that are in store for them, and you don't know how important these kids are to me. So take my job, I don't care. But you need to leave them alone – for good."

"Really, Ms. Kidd? Obviously these wild exaggerations are just a desperate attempt at keeping your job," he said, more of a growl than words. There was silence as Mr. Flint slowly pushed Daisy's hand away and looked to Teresa. "Ms. Madison, you've heard my recommendation. It would be in your best interest to take my offer, for the children's sake as well as yours."

Teresa stood up beside Daisy, let out a deep sigh, and pointed to the door. "I think it would be in your best interest to leave. Right. Now," she said.

Flint was obviously taken aback but didn't argue. Instead, he tipped his hat and said, "I'm not empowered to make this decision for you. Let me be clear that you are making a grave error, and with that, I'll bid you good day." He spun on his heels and headed towards the door, snapping his fingers at his entourage. "It's time we leave."

Marco stood with his hands clenched into tight fists, his whole body shaking with rage. "This isn't how it was supposed to be. You idiots are ruining everything." Before they could react, Marco revealed a small item, about the size of a soda can, and threw it hard at the ground. In an instant, a wave of energy billowed from where it landed, knocking over the coffee table along with Mr. Flint's cup of tea. Before the cup hit the floor, it froze mere inches from impact, its liquid contents suspended in air. Daisy, Zora, Nate, Teresa, Johann and Mr. Flint, were all stopped in mid-motion – frozen in time!

"This isn't how I wanted this to go," Marco said, his usually neat hair now hanging manically across his chiseled features. He took a pair of dark glasses from his vest pocket and put them on. They were just like Mr. Flint's, but with silver rims and elaborate symbols etched into the side guards. "I've planned this moment for so long. It was supposed to be far more…elegant." Somehow he was able to move freely through the time freeze, walking amongst them like so many department store mannequins. They were able to follow him with their eyes but unable to make even the slightest of movements. "You were supposed to fail the girl, Daisy, and leave her for me; confused, angry, and ready to follow my suggestion. Who knew you were actually any good at your job. Tsk, tsk."

He bent over to retrieve the item he had thrown from the floor, then held it out in front of Johann's frightened eyes. "Nice trick, huh Joe?" he laughed lightly. "Relative Time Grenade. Slows relative time for anyone in the blast radius, well, anyone not shielded that is. The

Balance does have some interesting toys that even the Laurel Society would love to get their greedy little hands on. Too bad really – I know you would have loved to examine some them." When he stood straight, he snapped his fingers in Flint's face, taking obvious joy in his frozen expression of bewilderment. "Didn't see this coming did you old boy. Truth be told neither did I, or at least not like this, but you've always said that seeing the future isn't an exact science, didn't you? I guess I'm going to have to improvise from here on in, won't I, Hobbs? Or should I say, Mr. Hammer."

Just then, they all noticed that Hobbs was still free to move.

"No need for code names now, Mr. Nail," he growled. "They were only meant to keep us hidden from the Watcher in case he saw us in one of his visions. Let's stop toying with them, get the girl and leave."

"Always to the point." Marco reached to the back of Zora's neck and pulled on her necklace, revealing the Master Gear. He held it up, allowing the light to catch on its peculiar surface. "These fools have no idea what was sitting right in front of them," he said. "The key to magic in this world, and the Adept who will unlock its secrets."

Marco pulled another instrument from his pocket, this one a long, thin rod of crystal. Affixed to the top was a copper dial that pulsed blue, sending similar pulses down the length of the crystal. "I guess it's time to go. Remember this day, all of you," Marco said menacingly. "Today is the day The Balance won."

Hobbs placed his hand on the crystal with Marco's, and in a flash they were gone, taking Zora with them.

MARCO FAULK
THE TAILOR

INTO THE DARKNESS

It took an hour for the magical effect to wear off. When time returned to normal, they all fell instantly to the ground, exhausted from holding awkward poses for so long. As feeling began to creep back into their limbs, fear crept into their hearts.

"What just happened?" Teresa said in a panic. Her hands were shaking. "Where did that man take Zora?"

"I don't know, Teresa, but we need to keep ourselves together. For Zora." Daisy's mind was racing, but she tried her best to keep her voice calm. "We'll figure this out."

"What's to figure out, Ms. Kidd?" Flint was up and gathering his men. "We've been betrayed, and I, for one, will not tolerate it. Daggers, we're returning to the chapter house. We'll gather our resources there and find these traitors!"

"Wait, you're leaving?" Daisy said as she moved to block the door. "Zora is with Marco. We have to find her. She's our main priority."

Flint raised his hand, motioning her aside. "Don't presume to tell me what is a priority, Ms. Kidd. These traitors will be apprehended, and Ms. Sparks returned," he said, "but you must see that this fiasco is on your head as well." Mr. Flint's voice was unnervingly calm. "You did not tell us about the girl's power, or about this artifact she carried, both of which are now in the hands of The Balance. You have botched this assignment completely." He then leaned towards her ear, so close she could feel his breath on her neck. "Just know I will make it my personal pleasure to make sure that your dismissal from the the Wardens is the least of your worries."

The remaining Daggers stood with their arms crossed behind their backs. "What are your orders, sir?"

"We need to return to the Chapter House and gather our resources," Flint said and pointed to Johann. "Mr. Epstein, gather up the rest of Ms. Spark's experiments. We need to see if we can find any clues in them." Lastly, he turned to Teresa. "We will find your niece and get to the bottom of this disaster, Ms. Madison. Zora may be headed for Shroudhurst Hospital, but you will at least get to say your goodbyes." With that, Flint and the

Daggers left through the front door, leaving the room in tense silence.

"Daisy, I'm so sorry," Johann said, nervously running his fingers through his hair. "I had no idea about Marco. I can't believe he…he lied to us, all of us, about everything."

"Is that it?" Nathan said, his voice quivering with fear and rage. He looked to Daisy. "They just leave without another word? Come'on D, you've got to help us. Where did he take Zora?"

Daisy had a thousand thoughts racing through her head at the moment, but the loudest of them was the last thing Zora had said to her before they entered the house. *Just in case the worst does happen, I trust you to know what to do with this.* Daisy pulled the journal from her pocket, and almost as if the girl's words were a premonition, she DID know what she had to do.

Daisy took Nate by the hand. "Do you trust me?" she said.

"Yes," Nate replied, without pause.

"Good, because we're going to find your sister." Daisy turned to Teresa. "I'm not going to stop until we get her back. You understand?" and Teresa nodded.

"How?" Johann looked confused. "The societies have been searching for The Balance for centuries, without any success – how are we supposed to find them?"

"The rest of the societies never had Johann Epstein on the case," Daisy said, taking her friend's hand. "I know you don't need this kind of trouble, but we need you. I need you…your help, that is."

"Do you even need to ask?" Johann said, his shoulders squared and his jaw set. "I'm in, but I don't know what help a Tinker is going to be. We don't even know where to start."

"We'll start here." Daisy handed the journal to him. Johann opened the book, and as he quickly leafed through it his eyes got wider and wider with each page.

"It's not possible," he whispered in breathless excitement. "This is the Rathmore journal. The same one that's been lost for decades. How did she…I mean… where did she…"

"That doesn't matter right now," Daisy replied, "this is our only clue to what The Balance wants with Zora. Somehow she knew it would be important, so I need you to work a miracle."

Johann flipped through the book frantically again, this time running his finger over the words on each page. "There is so much information in here, about his travels, his discoveries…"

"But what about The Balance, or Zora?" Nathan said. "Clues man! We need clues!"

Johann stopped and showed a page to them. On it was a drawing of the Master Gear, rendered perfectly in charcoal pencil, and beside it another drawing, this one of a massive gateway. There was a figure beside it for scale, showing the gate to be over eleven feet tall, and adorned in amazing carvings, much the same as those Daisy at seen in the observatory and the Well of Memory. "It says here," Johann read, "that the Master Gear is a crucial piece to this – something called the Gate of Nofret. Rathmore discovered it in Africa and moved it to the United States piece by piece in the early 1920s. He tried to assemble it, but something went… terribly wrong. To protect the world from some kind of danger, he dismantled it and hid this pivotal piece – The Master Gear. Without it, the Gate of Nofret is useless."

"Anything else?" Daisy asked. "There has to be something else."

"Yes. Apparently, Rathmore couldn't get the gate to work." Johann pushed his glasses up on his nose and read a particular entry again. "This is what he wrote:

After all my years of study and discovery, I was certain I was the one destined to bring this amazing construct to life and to feel the unfettered power of etherea from beyond the Fold. In my zeal to keep it out of the hands of the Thule and The Balance, I destroyed it, but I knew I could build it again. However, it was all in vain. Cruel pride and vainglory have blinded me to my own shortcomings. The Gate requires one of greater power than I – one truly adept in the Wonderous Science.'

"Zora?" Daisy felt the knot in the pit of her stomach. "They're going to use her to power the Gate of Nofret."

"There's more," Johann said gravely and read on:

'Without a strength beyond measure, the power of the gate would surely destroy any common practitioner. Even I faced my own death in activating it, and still feel the scars of my hubris until this day. I have wrought such suffering in the world, and I will spend the rest of my days repaying my debt to humanity.'

Teresa gasped. "I don't know what is going on here," she said, "but we need to find Zora before these men hook her up to this thing."

Before Daisy could reply, Nathan stopped them both, pointing at the box of items taken from the workshop. Underneath the machine parts, wires, and tools, something was moving. Johann had noticed as well, a small bird-shaped object, and he held his finger to his lips for silence. He crept closer, and suddenly the shape fluttered out into the air, landing on the arm of the couch.

"Amazing," Johann said, looking astonished at the bird, which in turn looked quizzically at the strange man before it. "How did this automaton activate itself? No one is controlling it."

"That's not an automa-whatever – that's Kuli!" Nate said, scooping the little metal bird up into his hands and holding him close. "I thought you would be hiding downstairs." Kuli rubbed his beak against Nathan's thumb lovingly before taking flight again. They all watched as it hovered before them, wings beating the air so fast they were a mere blur. He did a loop around the room, calling in a loud, metallic chirp.

"What's he doing?" Daisy said.

"Looking for Zora," Nate replied. As soon as he spoke, a smile of pure excitement came over his face. "Hey! Why don't we just follow Kuli?"

"Nathaniel Sparks, you're a genius!" Daisy cried, pulling Nate in for a big kiss on the cheek. "Your sister said the bird could follow her anywhere, didn't she?"

"Yeah. Use to make hide and seek with her way too easy."

Daisy buttoned her coat quickly and pulled her bowler down tight. "Joe, grab anything you think we could use out of those boxes. We're going to need more than just my beat up umbrella."

"On it," he replied, and dove up to his elbows in mechanical bits and pieces, stuffing some of the most interesting parts into the knapsack at his side.

"And what about me," Teresa said, looking deter-mined. "This is my family we're talking about. I'm not standing here while you chase this bird God know's where. I'm in this till the end, no matter how weird it gets."

"I was hoping you'd say that," Daisy said, "because we're going to need all the help we can get. I'm not going to lie to you, this will be dangerous."

Teresa grabbed her coat off the back of her chair. "Just try to stop me."

Kuli led them through the kitchen, down the stairs, and into the basement. Once there he tapped on the wall that concealed the entrance to the Secret Sanctum.

"I don't get it," Teresa said, "what are we doing down here?"

Nate pushed past the group and stood beside Daisy. "If you're coming along, Aunt T," he said, "you're just going to have to go with the flow. Oh, and try not to freak out every time something strange happens."

Daisy tapped a series of bricks, pulled hard on a jump rope that seemingly hung from a coat hook, and the doorway slid open. They all heard Teresa muffled gasp as Kuli led them down into the workshop.

"You guys have been busy," she said in a hushed voice.

The room looked different from the last time Daisy had been there. The shelves were almost bare, and the lights overhead were dark, save for a few near the entrance that gave the room an eerie blue glow. It made the space feel colder somehow – devoid of the spirit that had illuminated it before. Kuli landed on Zora's workbench and chirped loudly as he hopped around, motioning towards the large map that hung over the table.

"What now, Kuli?" Nathan asked. He watched as the bird hovered up to the map and pulled hard at its edge. "Zora use to obsess over this map," he said, moving closer, "but she never told me why."

"She said it was why she helped your aunt get this house," Daisy said, "something about tunnels that ran under Portland."

"That's it!" Johann almost giggled as he pulled the journal from under his arm and examined it again by the small amount of light in the room. "The journal mentions a series of tunnels that Rathmore used to move the gate in secret. It even shows his route."

At that moment, Kuli pulled hard on the map until it came loose from the wall, revealing a small panel set into the brick. There was a button at the center of the panel, the only part of it that wasn't covered in years of dust, and before anyone could stop him, Nathan slammed his hand down on it. They all heard a resounding click, followed by the grinding of something against the floor to their right. When it was finished, there was a dark opening where the wall had been.

"A secret passage IN the Secret Sanctum!" Nathan squealed, "Who saw that coming?"

Daisy peered down into the blackness. "It's another staircase, but it's hard to see how far it goes down…" While she stared into the gloom, Johann reached over and took her umbrella from under her arm, twisted the handle counter-clockwise, and tapped it hard against the wall. The tip of it instantly began to glow blue and give off small sparks of light that trailed off into the dark.

"You really don't read your items manual much, do you?" he said, smiling.

"Oh hush," she replied, only slightly embarrassed, "and somebody grab that map."

They moved quickly down the stairs into the tunnels, Kuli leading the way through the dark. It was quiet in those long forgotten passages, and the light emanating from Daisy's umbrella only made small patches of the way ahead visible. The dusty, stale air hung about them, dulling every sound and breath until the only thing they heard was the steady beating of their own hearts. They walked on, minutes turning into an hour, and an hour becoming two. Johann kept busy retooling Zora's inventions into items they could use if they ran into danger while Teresa kept her mind occupied by reading pages out of the journal as Nathan walked in front of her like a bodyguard. Daisy held the light aloft, keeping her eye on Kuli and checking the map periodically to make sure she kept her bearings. She feared if she got them lost down there in the gloom, they might just end up stuck in those tunnels permanently.

"I didn't say thank you, back there," Teresa said unexpectedly. Her voice was low, but she was close enough that it didn't take much to be heard. "You really stood up for us at the house. Your boss, Mr. Flint, doesn't look like the kind of guy to go up against, but you did, for me and the kids. I'm sorry that it cost you your job."

"It's ok," Daisy replied, breathing out a deep sigh. "It's kind of funny, really. I felt like I was finally starting to get good at looking after the kids. Well, except for watching Zora get whisked away by a guy I thought was pretty nice. Not my best moment."

"Well, you're making up for it now." Teresa touched her gently on the shoulder. "I can't judge anyway. Look at all the stuff I missed; there was a secret lab in my basement, and my niece is some kind of magic prodigy."

"I'm kind of magic too," Nate added.

"Really! Wow, I'm just terrible at this parenting thing. And on top of everything, I'm probably fired, so we've got that to deal with when we get back…"

"Shhhhh!" Nate held up his hand and stopped the group. "Do you hear that?"

Just ahead, the umbrella light fell on Kuli, now sitting quietly on a stack of old crates, and beside him stood an iron door, studded with bolts attaching it to the brick wall. It looked more like a submarine hatch, with a locking wheel in its center. As they got closer, Daisy could just make out the sound of voices on the other side.

THE GATE AND THE BALANCE

"Anybody have any bright ideas?" Daisy whispered to the group. The voices on the other side of the door sounded way off, but through that heavy iron material they could very well have been just a few feet away. "This is supposed to be a stealth mission. Nothing good is going to come from being seen as soon as we walk through the door."

Johann pressed his ear against the door. "They're nearby, but maybe we can use that to our advantage." He beckoned everyone in close. "Lets spring a little trap shall we?" he said, pulling out two of Zora's doormakers. "I've been tinkering with these in the tunnels, and I think they are just what we need." After Johann laid out his his plan, Daisy and Teresa stared at him in quiet shock while Nathan hopped back and forth on the balls of his feet, beaming with excitement.

"That is the most insane thing I've ever heard!" Teresa said, "I don't know if I should be impressed or horrified."

"Probably a little bit of both," Johann admitted, "but at this point, I can't see an alternative."

<hr />

On the other side of the bolted gateway, two Dagger guards stood in conversation.

"Any idea how long we're supposed to be down here?" one asked the other. "All the action is happening upstairs, and here we are babysitting the basement. Why do the Blades get to have all the fun?"

"Orders are orders." the other replied. "Besides, a little down time never hurt."

They heard a rattle from the portal door at the end of the hall. "What was that?" the first Dagger asked

The second leaned forward, cautiously looking down the hall. "Probably just a pressure shift on the other side." Suddenly there was another rattle, this time with a voice calling, "Help! Help! Is there someone there?" Together they made their way down the corridor, and with a turn of the wheel, unbolted the hatch, ready to spring at any intruder. They rushed to the opening, but all they saw was one woman leaning against the far wall.

"Thank God!" she squealed, limping towards them, "You've found me! I thought I'd be stuck down here forever."

"Don't move," the first guard demanded, poised to attack. "Who are you, and why are you here? These tunnels are private property."

"I'm sorry," Teresa limped closer, "I was just doing some treasure hunting, amateur obviously – this shady guy at the Saturday Market gave me this map here, and I should have known it was bogus. The man smelled like curry and bad cheese, so that should have been my first warning…"

"Quiet!" the other guard barked, stepping forward and igniting his gloves. They burned with a dull blue glow, casting their light on Teresa's frightened face. He held his hand level with her neck, just close enough that she could hear the sizzle of energy coursing through his fingers and smell ozone burning her sinuses. "You're lying," he said. "No one has a map that leads to these tunnels. Who sent you? Speak quickly before something bad happens to you – far worse than being lost in the dark."

"Funny you should mention that," Teresa said, and dove quickly to the ground. Hovering cloaked above the guards, Daisy, Nathan and Johann threw two of Zora's triangular doormakers at the ground beneath the Dagger's feet. They instantly opened, forming large gateways into a swirly, starry space, sucking both of the men into them. They barely managed a yelp before the gateways snapped shut to the sound of rushing air.

"HA! Not so scary now, are ya!" Nate hollered, pointing where the guards once stood. When his feet touched down, he did a victory dance around the now dormant doormakers. "You guys should have let me take care of em'."

"Quiet Nate! Let's keep the celebrating to a minimum," Daisy said as she landed and reached down to Teresa to help her up. "We don't know who else is in earshot. Stealth, remember!"

Nate gave her a silent salute.

Johann picked up the doormakers and examined them. "They worked! Incredible!"

"I'm ok too, by the way," Teresa said.

"Oh Teresa, I'm so sorry. I didn't expect them to get so aggressive so quickly."

She patted him on his arm with a shaky hand. "That's alright, Joe. One thing you could do for me, though – in the next plan you come up with, how about making someone else the bait? Someone that has magic, maybe?"

He nodded his head. "I think I can do that."

The hallway was dim beyond the iron door, but as they moved forward Daisy could make out the shapes of artwork and artifacts adorning the walls — austere portraits of men and women with amazing wonderous items she had never even heard of, let alone seen. Their eyes seemed to follow them as they moved past their portraits flanked by tools and weapons mounted on the walls beside them, each from times ancient and obscure. As the group crept down the corridors, Kuli leading the way, they found themselves moving into a large room lit by mounted wall sconces, the air smelling of machine oil and brass cleaner. Daisy instantly knew where they were.

"We're in the lab?" she said, a shocked squeak in her voice. She looked over her shoulder at Johann. "Did you know about this? The tunnels and that door?"

"More importantly, did you know about The Balance?" Nathan said, giving Johann a threatening look. Kuli landed on his shoulder, cocking his head to glare at Johann as well.

"No! Of course not! Yes, this is where I work, but we were only allowed in this room, and sworn not to wander around in the mansion…" Johann groaned as he realized what he'd said, "it's all supposed to be secret."

"What mansion?" Daisy said. "Joe, where exactly are we?"

He hesitated for a moment before answering. "This is Rathmore Mansion, the former home of Elias W. Rathmore. We, the Tinker-Tailors I mean, have been studying his work and artifacts in hopes of better understanding the wealth of knowledge he kept stored here. He hoarded years worth of research, journals, and discoveries that we could scarcely imagine. Rathmore never trusted the Laurel Society, and in turn, the Society never trusted a practitioner of his power and skill operating outside of their control, so they kept their distance from each other. Now, with the problems facing practitioners today, the Society needs to know what he knew. So after I finished my training, I was recruited to come here in secret to start studying and cataloging everything that's been found. Truth be told, I'm not supposed to be telling you any of this."

"Why, Joe? Afraid I'm going to spill the beans? Huh!" Daisy felt her face flushing red, and she tried her best to keep her voice as level as possible. "I'm tired of all the secrets and half truths. What else do you know that I don't?"

"Nothing. I'm as in the dark about all of this as you. I've just been doing what I was told until now. I assumed we were here to be closer to Rathmore's work, and the fact that no one comes around here was kind of a bonus. The house has a bit of reputation."

"Is it haunted? Oh please say it's haunted," Nathan said with glee.

"That's absurd. There's no such thing as ghosts," Johann replied.

"Really?" Teresa said, with a well-executed eye roll. "A guy that opened two pocket universes just three minutes ago says ghosts are absurd? How's that for perspective?"

"All I know is that things are known to happen near the house and graveyard on the grounds. Weird sounds. Strange lights. The Society has been keeping it all quiet for years, and the house has never been sold or lived in by anyone since Rathmore died – not until we came. For the past year, things have been really tense around here. Something has the Society scared and scrambling, and it's definitely not ghosts."

They made their way to the door leading out of the lab, but before Daisy could touch the knob, Johann reached out and stopped her.

"Wait," he said and pointed at the gold crest on the door. "You need to tap that with your ring. It's still set to open at the Chapter House."

"Thanks, Joe. That would have been really awkward," she said. Daisy tapped the crest three times and then reached for the doorknob again. When it opened, there was no twisting starscape on the other side. Instead, there was another long, dimly lit corridor, similarly decorated with portraits and assorted artifacts. Just as they started down the hall, the door at the far end swept open, and in walked three Daggers, and the one in the lead was Mr. Hobbs.

"HEY YOU! STOP WHERE YOU ARE!" Hobbs bellowed, igniting his gloves.

"What now, what now, what now!" Johann cried, frantically rummaging through his bag.

"Now… you hold onto something." Daisy reached into her pocket and pulled out the watch. As soon as the Daggers were halfway down the hall, she activated the Splendid Machine, and in an instant, the room began to turn onto its side, furniture and portraits lifting free from the floor and walls. Gravity was gone, or at least was suddenly in a very finicky mood.

"How is this supposed to help?" Teresa cried, holding for dear life to a marble bust of some very dower looking woman.

"I'm not sure!" Daisy yelled, trying to find something to grab onto. It took a second or two but they quickly noticed how she was moving. "Everybody, you can swim through the air! Try pushing off from the walls." Behind her, Daisy heard the metallic sound of Nathan's dynamo fists activating.

"Oh yeah! Now it's time to play!" he yelled, and bounded down the hall, jumping from wall to wall and over floating tables and assorted weapons, followed closely behind the shimmering of Kuli's wings beating effortlessly in the suspended gravity. Daisy didn't waste any time, leaving Teresa and Johann so she could back up the impulsive Mr. Sparks. The Daggers had regained their bearings, and Hobbs launched himself in Nathan's direction, hands extended like glowing claws. Nate saw him and kicked off of a large vase, barely missing the crackling weapons. Hobbs barreled into the wall, sending small trails of electricity arcing across the space on impact. His next swing fared better, slashing through Nate's coat then catching him by the collar. Nate delivered a hard punch to his midsection, but it only made him angrier.

"You little pest! I'm gonna…" POW!! A blazing arch of blue smashed into the Daggers outstretched arm! It was Daisy, wielding her umbrella and rebounding off the wall for another strike. Before she could land it, though, the last Dagger grabbed hold of her ankle.

"Get off!" she slammed her umbrella down hard, but the Dagger guard caught it in mid swing. While she wrestled with him, she could see Nate having it out with another Dagger just behind her, the sound of hard blows seeming to shake the very air around them. "Nathan, get Johann and Teresa out of here!" Before she could say another word, the effect of the Splendid Machine wore off, sending them all crashing hard to the ground. She lay there, dazed and aching. Even though the magic effect had ended, the room still felt like it was spinning, and by the time she'd recovered, Teresa, Johann, and Nate were all captured.

"When I'm done with you lot, you're going to wish you had never been born," Hobbs said as he stood over them. He sounded funny since his nose was broken, but the look of pure menace in his eyes was anything but funny.

"Enough of this!" a voice called out from the far end of the corridor. "They aren't to be harmed." A figure walked confidently through the doorway, umbrella held smartly under her arm, and the steady click, click, click of her heels reverberating through the now still space. Daisy looked up to see Stephanie Love standing over her with that same quiet, condescending smile she always wore. "Marco wants them brought along. He wants them to witness the big event."

"You're a part of this?" Daisy said, her voice faltering. She was literally shaking with anger and would have cried if it weren't for that smile on Stephanie's face. "I can't believe you! All of that time, filling my head with all that talk about tradition and the duty of The Wardens, and here you were a traitor all along."

"Oh, poor sweet Daisy," Stephanie crooned. She reached down and cupped Daisy's chin in her pristine hands. "I meant everything I said. All of it. But this, well, this is about more than any of that. Something far grander."

"What then?" Daisy growled. "What could be so important that you would turn your back on everything we believe in?"

"The future, dear girl. Of course." Stephanie stood and motioned to the Daggers. "Hobbs, have your men bring them. They wouldn't want to miss the show."

Daisy, Teresa, Nate and Johann were led out of the mansion through the main hall, but not before their captors took Daisy's bowler hat and umbrella, and Nathan's dynamo fists. Their hands were bound as well, even Teresa's. The mansion was truly immense, but they could barely appreciate any of the grandeur in their current predicament. Once outside, Daisy could see the moon, half-obscured by clouds, and smell the wet pavement beneath her feet. She chanced a look back at the facade of Rathmore Mansion. For all it's size and opulence, there was something lonely about the place, and at that moment it felt as if those dark windows above her head were looking down on her judgingly. *I've failed them. I've failed them all*, she thought.

Across the main drive of the mansion stood a long, wrought iron fence that disappeared left and right into the surrounding trees. In its center was a double gate, crowned with an elaborate "R" set into the twisting metal work. Beyond, there was just enough moonlight for Daisy to make out the tops of gray headstones and mausoleums in the evening fog. The Daggers marched them all through the gate, Stephanie Love leading the way. They followed a worn, gravel path through the graveyard until they came to a squat stone crypt. Above the door were etched the words, Rathmore: Keeper of Ways. Standing beneath the inscription in the shadowy entrance was Marco Faulk impatiently sliding his shoe across the marble step.

"What an unexpected surprise," he said, adjusting his mirrored spectacles and giving them all an unnerving smile. "Welcome to the new age of magic."

E.W. RATHMORE
THE INNOVATOR

AN ADEPT'S POWER

"**Y**ou better not have hurt my sister," Nathan growled, glaring up at Marco with pure menace. "You have no idea how hard I'll come down on you if even one hair on her big ole' head is out of place. You got me? One hair!"

"Is that so, Mr. Sparks? Well, we wouldn't want that, would we?" Marco snickered, his voice cool and smooth. He looked very different in his black frock coat and gray vest, embroidered with small silver scales. He carried a silver-handled umbrella, and his hair, which Daisy had once thought so nice, was slicked back making him look very cold and austere. "You'll be happy to know that she is fine…for now. But wait, I'm getting ahead of myself." He motioned to the Dagger guards to bring them along as he entered into the crypt. Inside, the air was stale and smelled of dead leaves and mildew, and all around them were rectangular panels, each with names and dates etched into their surfaces. At the far end of the cold space was an altar, on which sat an odd statue – a hand holding aloft a globe. Carved deep into the gray stone were the words CREDO IN STUPOREM, the same as Daisy had seen back at the Rookery.

"What is this place?" she whispered, and Marco turned to address her.

"Welcome to the last resting place of one of the greatest practitioners of the Wonderous Science the world has ever known, or not known in his case. Elias Rathmore was a pioneer, and a visionary." Marco placed his hand on the globe and began to touch individual countries in a particular order. "He traveled the world over, collecting knowledge, but even with all he learned, The Laurel Society never saw him as anything but a problem – an outlier and a disgrace. If only those fools had known how truly wrong they were." As he finished the sequence, there was a sharp click followed by the sound of gears turning. When the sound ground to a stop, the globe quickly split in two and twisted away to reveal a stairway beneath the altar. "Come, all of you. The answers you seek are down there," he pointed to the stair, "down in the dark."

The passage wound down into the earth, and Daisy was glad to see there were lights positioned every few yards. As if climbing down a stairway in a graveyard weren't bad enough, doing it in complete darkness while shackled would have been just too much. Behind her, she could hear Teresa's panicked breaths and Johann trying his best to calm her. Daisy kept Nathan close to her, and even though he was putting on his best warrior face, she could feel him making sure to stay just behind her arm. Kuli was nowhere to be found, and she hadn't seen the little bird since they had been captured. For some reason, knowing he was still out there gave Daisy a small glimmer of hope.

When the group came to the end of the stairs, the passage opened up into a tall chamber. It had to be over thirty feet high, she thought, cut into the soft stone beneath the manor grounds. The ceiling was supported by six wide columns, carved in a similar fashion to the reliefs from the Well of Memory – even the scenes they depicted were familiar. Between each column stood a menacing looking statue, four in total, of men in ancient armor, each holding a spear in its outstretched claw. Beneath their feet, the floor was a mosaic of swirling patterns, drawing Daisy's eye across the immense space.

That was when she saw what Marco had obviously brought them there to see. At the far end of the chamber was a raised dais with steps leading up, and at the center of the circle stood a tall archway. It was the most amazing thing she had ever seen, composed of a stone that had blue veins coursing through it, each pulsing with some inner power. Even though it appeared to be hewn from solid rock, this was no crudely made form – instead, it was quite complex with fittings of copper and jade covering its surface. The front of the gateway was made to resemble a woman's face with high cheekbones, a full mouth, and open eyes that gave off an astonishing glow. Standing there before it was Zora Sparks, the blue light of the gateway seeming to surround her, coiling and coursing its way into her tiny frame. She didn't turn to greet them. Instead, she stood there, held in the thrall of the powerful artifact.

"ZORA!" Teresa yelled. She tried to break free from the Dagger's grip. It was only then that Daisy noticed they weren't the first to arrive in the chamber. Out of the shadows came three dark figures with bone white masks, their inky weapons swirling anxiously around their arms. The Blades of the Balance had been waiting for them. Daisy kept her eyes on Zora, and could have sworn she saw her mouth the words, *Help me.*

"What's wrong with Zora?" Nathan pleaded. The guards forced them all down before the dais and onto their knees. Daisy could hear Johann groan as he came down hard on the tiles while Teresa wrapped her shackled arms around Nathan and held him close. In front of them, Stephanie Love stood watching the incredible scene with a satisfied smile on her face.

"She can't hear you," Marco said, "she's connected to it now. Ms. Sparks is witnessing something that no one has witnessed for over 3000 years." He held his arms wide. "Behold! The Gate of Nofret – the greatest magical artifact ever discovered. Beyond this door lies the birthplace of all magic. A place known only as The Fold." He took one step up onto the dais, reaching towards Zora and a small wisps of the blue energy glided through his fingers. "It's from there that all etherea flows. Long ago, The Wonderous Masters tried to change the destiny of the world by blocking that flow – by hampering the abilities of anyone who would ever practice the Wonderous Science. People like me."

"You don't know what you're doing!" Daisy cried. "The Masters made this thing for a reason!"

"The Masters were pompous fools," Marco screamed, losing his thin facade of composure. "They even constructed this gate to only respond to the touch of a true Adept – a practitioner with abilities like their own." He clenched his hand, growing eerily still. "Do you have any idea what it is like to have potential, real potential, for power and status, but at every turn to be told that you were never meant for it? To be relegated to being nothing more than a cog in a system not of your making?" He pointed to the Blades, the Dagger, and to Stephanie Love. "We servants of The Balance know what it is to be blocked from achieving our true potential. Ever since I was a child, my parents were members of the Society. They knew that my abilities would only ever allow me to be a Tinker-Tailor, left to repair wonderous items but never allowed to use them, but I had much bigger dreams. I was Ms. Sparks' age when I discovered I was actually a Watcher – gifted with the ability to see the future, but not to a degree that would allow me to join their ranks. I knew I was capable of so much more, and that someday I would prove it to them, the Society, and the world. That day is today. The gate will be open, and the world will be grateful for it."

Daisy glanced behind her to check on the others when something caught her attention. A small shimmer, like light reflecting off of burnished metal. She looked down and saw Kuli, hard at work on Teresa and Nathan's bindings. Nathan even chanced a smile, but quickly motioned her to look away.

Just then, there was a surge of energy from the gate, and the blue light in the room reached a new brightness, followed closely by a rushing sound that quickly filled the room.

"She's done it. The flow has reached its peak. It's almost time, Marco," Stephanie said and signaled to the guards. "She's drawn through enough etherea. When the door opens we'll have to be at a safe distance. Get the girl."

While Ms. Love and Marco talked, Daisy could feel Johann cut the bindings from around her wrists. "We need to do something," he whispered.

Daisy reached into her pocket and felt the welcome weight of the golden watch. "Thank goodness they didn't take it," she said. She turned to Johann and whispered just loud enough for him to hear her over the roar of the gate. "I have a plan."

On the dais, Marco removed his glasses, laid his umbrella to the side, and turned to Ms. Love. "Plans have changed, my dear," he said cooly. "The young Zora has untrained power, but her emotions are too raw, too uncontrolled. There is no way she has the strength to pull herself away from the flow of power from the gate – so, let's see this as an opportunity. We will leave her to her fate, and allow her to open the gate as wide as she can. This world will be flooded with magical energy like it was in ancient times. Imagine the abilities that will open to us! Unfortunately, I'm afraid it will be the end of Ms. Sparks."

Stephanie stood frozen, the light from the gate highlighting the disbelief on her face. "That was never the plan," she said over the roar. "We were supposed to open the flow of etherea, not open the gate! We have no idea what that will do to the world, not to mention the girl. Was this what you had in mind all along, Marco?"

"Don't you see? We have a chance here to change everything," he replied, "to finally rise above all those practitioners that have held us back. I'm not wasting it – I've come too far." Before Stephanie could react, Marco place his hand on Zora's shoulder. In an instant, the glow from the gate became immense, sending tendrils of etherea reaching out into the chamber. Everything was awash in its power.

"Follow my lead," Daisy said, and held up the Splendid Machine. With one click of the watch, the stone guards between the columns, once silent and still, pulled themselves free from the ground with a resounding crack. Moving with unexpected speed for giants of stone and iron, they turned to face the Blades and Daggers, spears held at the ready. "ATTACK!!" she yelled. Nathan and Kuli jumped into action, Johann not far behind them. The guards had taken Nate's gauntlets, but as he leaped over the nearest Blade's head, a five-foot long bow staff appeared in his hand, like a magician's wand at a kids magic show. Once in his hand, he brought it down with a resounding crack before the Blade even saw it coming.

"Come'on, Joe!" he yelled, "we can't let these stone guys have all the fun!"

Johann didn't have time to reply, as he was fending off a Dagger with what appeared to be some kind of jump rope, the length of which blazed bright yellow with each swing.

Daisy knew right away where she was needed. "Come'on Teresa," she said, grabbing her hand. "Let's get your niece." Together they made their way up the steps of the dais, battered by the rush of wind and energy. When they looked up, however, they found themselves face to face with Stephanie Love. Both her hands rested on the handle of her umbrella, and her golden hair whipped around her face as if it were alive. Daisy looked back at Teresa. "Get to Zora," she said, "she's going to need you."

"What am I supposed to do?" Teresa yelled back, but Daisy had already let go of her hand.

"Stephanie, you need to move out of our way," Daisy said, half demanding, half pleading. "I don't know why you are a part of this, but Marco needs to be stopped. Can't you see that?"

Stephanie tilted her head and smiled primly. "I always knew you were going to be trouble for me," she replied, "and now here we are. I couldn't stop this if I wanted to. The process has already begun. This wasn't what The Balance had planned, but it will have to do, and I'm not about to let you and your band of misfits get in our way." In a blinding flash, Stephanie attacked, her umbrella blazing to life. Daisy barely sidestepped the first blow but felt it slash past the tip of her nose. The next one came fast. Stephanie spun around, slamming Daisy hard in the stomach and sending her sliding across the dais. She came in quickly for a third and final blow, but found her weapon blocked by another. Daisy had retrieved Marco's silver-handled umbrella from the ground.

"I thought we were friends," Daisy said, and in one fluid motion she swept Stephanie's leg out from under her. In seconds they were both back on their feet, their weapons at the ready. They clashed back and forth in the growing maelstrom, each in perfect step with the other. For years, Daisy had been afraid of Stephanie, her reputation for being the best and brightest of the Wardens, but in that moment, there in the glow of the Gate of Nofret, she didn't care. All that mattered was Zora. Their umbrellas were alive, blazing swords sweeping this way and that like a dancing moonbeams, but the longer they fought, the more Daisy knew she was outmatched.

"You can't win here, lil' flower," Stephanie cried, their weapons straining against each other. "You might as well give up now. I've always been better than you, smarter, the very picture of a Warden. We both know that no matter what you do, you can never be me."

With the last of her strength, Daisy kicked off of the ground, gliding high into the air, then came down hard with her umbrella. There was a swath of light and a distinct ring as the silver tip of her weapon cracked the stone of the dais. When she looked up, Stephanie was on the ground with the ragged cut from her hairline to the base of her cheek. Daisy rose and stood over her former mentor. "Truth be told," she said, just loud enough to be heard over the growing tumult, "I never wanted to be you. I really never liked you that much." Stephanie didn't reply. Instead, she stumbled back down the steps, cradling her wounded face in her hands, and retreated into the shadows of the chamber.

<hr />

Daisy turned and headed back to the gate through the rushing wind and swirling eddies of sparkling blue. As she moved closer, she could hear Teresa's voice calling into the wind, "Zora! Zora, baby can you hear me!" Daisy could see three silhouettes; one was Marco, moving like he was caught in a hurricane; the other was Teresa, and standing in front of them all was Zora, perfectly still as if she couldn't feel any of it. Daisy could see the gate more clearly now, and what she saw took her breath away. The image of the woman had both her eyes and mouth open, and beyond the opening was a swirling infinite space, a twisting cauldron of color so rich that it baffled the mind.

"I can't wake her!" Teresa yelled, tears streaming down from her eyes. "Help me!"

Daisy had no idea what to do. She didn't dare touch Zora after seeing what had happened to Marco. "Marco," she whispered, "he's the key!" Daisy moved closer to him, trying her best to avoid making contact. As she came closer, she could hear his voice mixed in with the roar. He was repeating something; *So much power, so much power.* "MARCO! You have to let her go," Daisy yelled, "it's too much for you to take!"

"TOO MUCH!" Marco turned sharply towards Daisy, and the face she saw staring back at her was barely recognizable. The etherea was burning him from the inside, but there was a broad smile on his face. "You haven't seen what I've seen," he croaked. "There are other worlds beyond this opening – power unheard of, all for the taking. I must have it! I MUST HAVE IT ALL!" Without another word, Marco released Zora and dove into the swirling maelstrom of the gate. As he passed its boundaries, his body exploded into a million points of light, then simply faded away. The force of blast knocked Zora, Daisy, and Teresa back to the stairs of the dais, and there they lay in a heap.

Teresa was the first to move, crawling to her niece's side. When Daisy finally stirred, she saw Teresa cradling Zora in her arms.

"Zora? Sweetheart, can you hear me?" she whispered into her ear, rocking her gently. "You need to wake up and stop scaring me. I'm not built for this kind of drama."

There was a tense moment of silence, and Daisy found herself holding her breath.

And then, Zora spoke, softly but with that tang of attitude that was distinctly her. "I don't know about that, Aunt T," she groaned, "you're kind of a drama queen yourself."

"HALLELUJAH!" Teresa wrapped her arms around her niece's neck so tightly she could have squeezed all the breath out of her. "Don't you ever do that to me again, you hear? Eyes all crazy and glowing! You almost gave me a heart attack!"

Zora squeezed her in return. "See what I mean?" she said breathlessly. "Drama queen."

Daisy crawled over to them both, wrapping her arms around their shoulders and said, "You had us really scared, Zoe. Not sure what you have planned for an encore."

"We're not done yet," Zora replied and pointed at the gate. "The Master Gear is still set in the doorway. They made me put it there, and we need to get it out."

"Seriously!" Teresa said, looking beyond exhausted. "We just got you away from that thing, and now you want to go back up there?"

"Aunt T, if we don't the gate will never close," Zora said as she painfully stood, "the power from The Fold will burn everything here to atoms. I think it's the reason Rathmore dismantled it."

"So how are we supposed to get the gear?" Daisy said, standing at her side.

Zora smiled. "Do you still have that watch?"

They found Johann and Nathan not too far away, sitting exhausted in the shadow of a motionless stone warrior, amongst the wreckage of the other three. There were two Dagger guards lying unconscious a few feet from them, and no sign of the rest. The Blades were gone as well, having all escaped with Ms. Love after Marco disappeared, but one of their weapons still protruded from the chest of the last stone warrior. When Zora, Daisy, and Teresa came running up to meet them, both Joe and Nate had proud smiles on their soot-stained faces.

"Zora!" Nathan yelled, giving his big sister a hug. He was laughing, but it was easy enough for Daisy to see the tears in his eyes. "I knew you were going to be ok, I just knew it! Takes more than some pretty boy with fancy shades to beat you."

Zora and Teresa hugged him as hard as they could. "Of course I'm ok," Zora said in a very thin impression of annoyance, "who's supposed to keep you out of trouble if I'm not around?"

"Um, I think you actually got me into most of this trouble," he replied.

Daisy grabbed Johann and squeezed him as well. He replied with a wince and a groan, but she still held him for a moment. There really weren't any words that could capture how glad she was to see him, so all she said was, "That was something, wasn't it?" He just quietly laughed, but a sudden rush of air, followed by a flash of light quickly reminded them of the danger they were still in.

"I'm not really sure," Nathan said, pointing at the swirling havoc of the gate, "but I think you guys made it worse."

"We need Daisy's watch," Zora said, "I think she can use it to stop the power surges long enough for me to get the Master Gear."

Johann's face was the very picture of dread. "Are you both insane? There is no way that is going to work," he said, shaking his head. "The vortex has grown too powerful! In these conditions, there's no way of knowing how it will be affected. You already said that it works differently near the gear."

"Right now it's our only option," Daisy said.

"Alright. I hope you both have something resembling a plan."

Zora looked up at the gate, her mind making calculations faster than ever before. "We need a stabilizer. Something that can hold or siphon off the energy just long enough to counteract the effect on the watch. But what?"

"I know, I know!!" Nathan reached into Johann's bag and pulled out the last three doormakers. "Will these work?"

"My brother's a genius!" Zora yelled. She took them, examining the changes had been made. "Is this your work?" she said, turning to Johann. "Nice." She gathered them up and quickly made her way back to the foot of the dais, the rest of the group following close behind. The gateway was nearly fully open, and time was running out.

"You do realize that if this works, we'll lose the Master Gear," Johann said to Zora. "All that wonderous magic, gone forever?"

Zora pointed at the gate. "I think we're way passed that, don't you?

He didn't answer. Instead, he grabbed Daisy's arm. "Ms. Sparks has a very dry sense of humor," he said, checking the settings on the Splendid Machine one more time. "You'll only have a few minutes to make this work. If you're caught in the flow when the watch stops…"

Daisy silenced him with a kiss on the cheek. "I know. Stop worrying so much." She then looked to Zora. Her hands were shaking a bit. "You ok?" she said, the watch at the ready.

"More or less," Zora replied.

"That's not very reassuring."

"I'm still working out all of the angles."

Daisy took her hand. "Sweety, there's a point when you just have to stop considering things and trust that you're ready."

"I don't know about that, but I trust you." With one last glance back at Teresa, Nate, and Johann, Zora took Daisy's hand and squeezed. "On three. One. Two. Three!"

Daisy clicked the watch, and instantly found herself and Zora surrounded by a sea of light. It moved like it were alive, twisting and turning in waves of blue, red, and dappled purple, pushing against her chest like a sea current. Daisy fought through it with all her might, even though she could barely see past the blinding radiance. As her strength left, she could just make out Zora's silhouette ahead of her. She was reaching into the starry expanse that lay ahead – then, just as quickly as it had began, the light ended.

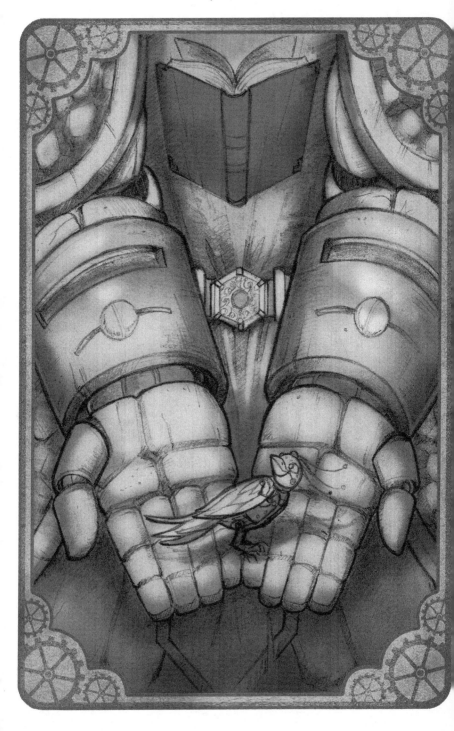

THE FUTURE OF MAGIC

When the Laurel Society finally arrived at Rathmore Manor, they went right to work rooting out their enemies. Most of the rogue Daggers were rounded up within a matter of minutes, while some were caught fleeing from the grounds. Mr. Flint stood upon the grand marble steps of the mansion, supervising the work and dispatching Stewards and Wardens to search the surrounding area for any that might have escaped.

"Leave no stone unturned," he bellowed, pointing at a small group of Stewards still searching the nearby graveyard, "and I mean that literally." Two of Flint's remaining loyal Daggers came bursting through the mansion doors. Hanging between them was Mr.

Hobbs, barely conscious after his run in with his former colleagues.

"Hello boss," he croaked through his swollen jaw, "funny running into you here."

"This whole situation is a great many things, none of them funny," Flint said, his voice like cold steel. "You will pay for your treachery, Mr. Hobbs, but first you tell me everything you know about The Balance. I have no problem keeping you in the deepest, darkest hole until you do. Take him away." Flint could barely hide his satisfaction watching Hobbs dragged away with a look of abject fear on his face.

From across the front drive, Mr. Hawk came running past the other Stewards, reaching the foot of the manor steps red and out of breath. "Sir, we've found something," he wheezed, pointing back towards the graveyard.

"Well come on man, out with it!" Flint growled.

Mr. Hawk took a second to catch his breath, then rattled off, "there's a secret passage under the Rathmore crypt leading to a chamber. I'm pretty sure you're going to want to see what's down there."

When Mr. Flint and his men made their way into the cavernous chamber, the first thing they noticed, sitting amidst the mayhem and destruction, were Daisy, Zora,

Nathan, Johann, and Teresa, laughing hysterically. Even Kuli was prancing and chirping excitedly on Zora's shoulder. They were all covered from head to toe in dust, their clothes were torn, and each of them looked as if they had been through a tornado, but they were laughing even as two Stewards bandaged and ran tests on each of them.

"What is the meaning of this?" Flint said, walking carefully over the rumble. He abruptly dismissed the Stewards.

"We just saved the world. You're welcome," Zora said then fell into her brother's arms in a fit of giggles.

"Yes sir," Daisy continued, barely keeping it together, "it's too bad you missed it!"

Flint looked less than amused, and growled, "Someone needs to give me a report of the situation immediately, or I swear…"

Luckily Johann was able to get control of himself. "I'm sorry sir," he snickered, "I think we've been affected by the etherea. It should wear off in a little bit. To put the whole thing succinctly, we won."

"I'm afraid more details will be required, Mr. Epstein."

Between the five of them, they were able to recount everything that had happened after Mr. Flint left Teresa's house, from the tunnels to the mansion and eventually the showdown with Stephanie Love and Marco at the gate. By the time they were done, Flint was almost speechless.

"So...I'm assuming the artifact is no longer a danger," he said, looking up to the top of the dais. The gate stood there, humming with energy from beyond, the eyes of Nofret's majestic face still open and glowing blue. "We need to know for sure if this object will be causing any more problems."

Zora held out her hand, and resting in her palm was the Master Gear. It's surface looked worn and brittle, it's once brilliant shine was now seared and blackened. "I don't think that you have to worry about that," she said confidently. In one motion, she crushed the gear, sprinkling the pieces at Mr. Flint's feet. "The gate is stable. It's not completely closed, but we stopped it from opening all the way."

Mr. Flint stood there in astonished silence, but just over his shoulder they all noticed the huge smile on Mr. Hawk's face, as well as the rest of Stewards, Daggers, and Wardens that had gathered in the chamber, and before long they all broke out into a huge round of applause. Daisy stood, as did Teresa and Johann, wrapping their arms around the small shoulders of Zora and Nate. All of the faces around them beamed, and they couldn't help but feel a swell of pride wash over them all.

"Silence," Mr. Flint eventually said, holding up a hand to the crowd. "Back to work, if you please! We need to gather all of this for study and records, and I won't have you missing a single piece of important evidence." As the Society members returned to their tasks, Mr. Flint turned again to address Zora, Daisy, and Nate. "This was good work, all of you," he said begrudgingly. "Although I had my doubts, you've proven yourselves today. With a little training and discipline, you may become passable members of the Laurel Society."

Instantly, Zora's smile disappeared. "So you want us now," she said. Her eyes narrowed, "after we saved the day. Just a few hours ago you were saying we were too dangerous, and making plans to send me off, and here you are trying to be nice all of a sudden?"

Flint tried again. "Well yes. I made assumptions about you and your brother…"

"And Daisy. Don't forget Daisy," Nathan added.

"… and Ms. Kidd."

"…and Kuli! Don't forget Kuli." Nate held the bird up on his finger right in front of Mr. Flint's nose, who tried his best to ignore him.

"As I was saying, based on how you handled yourselves today, I believe allowances can be made. You have an understanding of this artifact that no one else has. We could use you, and with your commitment to the Laurel Society, Ms. Kidd would be allowed back to the Wardens, of course."

Zora looked at Daisy. "What do you think?" she said. "This would mean you got your job back."

Daisy placed her hands on Zora's shoulders. "Seriously? You're always so sure of yourself, I'm surprised you're asking me what I think."

"Of course I want to know what you think," Zora said. "You're our Warden, right? I don't want that to change."

Daisy turned to Teresa, and Johann and Nathan, each of them nodding as she looked to them. She pulled Zora close and whispered, "That's never going to change, no matter what decision you make."

Zora breathed out a heavy sigh, smiled, and turned back to Flint. "I'm going to kindly deny your request, Mr. Flint. My family needs me. Besides, there isn't anything you can offer."

Even behind his dark glasses, Flint's eyes almost blazed with anger. "I'm only going to ask nicely once," he said, but before another word was said, a voice grabbed all of their attention.

"Once will be quite enough, Mr. Flint." Down the steps into the chamber came Ms. Mizner led by Mr. Porter. "These young people will not be hitching themselves to you and the Society right now. I think Ms.

Sparks and her brother's abilities warrant … special accommodations."

"Ms. Mizner," Flint said, " please, do tell?"

Mildred made her way deftly over the rubble with Porter's help, then stood toe to toe with Mr. Flint. "I was thinking independent study under the protection of Daisy, of course. Zora is fully capable of learning more on her own, considering everything that's happened today. We could even facilitate her lab at the Rookery."

"What if I refuse?" Flint murmured.

"You'll have to deal with us," Nate replied, crossing his arms and giving his best warrior stare.

Mildred couldn't help but let out a laugh that filled the chamber. "I wouldn't mess with this one, Flint. He may be the most talented Dagger the Society has ever seen. Well, it looks like things are all settled. You are going to be busy tonight, Arthur. You better get to it. Porter and I will make sure they get home ok."

Mr. Porter did a sharp salute. "Yes ma'am," he said. With that, Ms. Mizner lead them towards the exit of the chamber, leaving Mr. Flint and the rest of the Society members behind.

On the steps leading up to the graveyard, Teresa said, "Thanks for that. I'm sorry, this may sound silly, but who are you again?"

"I'm a friend. Right Zora?"

"Yes, ma'am," she replied, but then got quiet for a moment. "Everybody, I'm sorry for putting you all in danger," she said quietly, "and for making our lives so difficult. Aunt T., you lost your job for me. I'm sorry for that too."

Teresa grabbed her and hugged her tight, then pulled Nathan in as well. "After all of this crazy, you're talking about my job? Who cares! I'm just glad you guys are okay and we're together.

"About your job," Ms. Mizner said, "you worked for a hotel, yes? I run a kind of boarding house for former professionals with, let's just say 'special interests.' We could use someone with your talents."

"Wow. Wow! You're serious, right?"

"If I'm lyin' I'm dyin'."

Teresa was ecstatic. "That's great! Sounds good kids?"

"Perfect!" Nate said.

"Wonderful. Now since you've had a perilous night, why don't you all come back with me to the Rookery? We're having a roast, followed by a rousing game of checkers."

Teresa looked confused, but Zora patted her on the back. "You're in for some wonderful surprises, Aunt T."

Zora looked back one more time at the gate, but Daisy laid a hand on her shoulder, "You've got plenty of time for those secrets, Ms. Sparks," she said in a soothing voice. "Your adventures are only just beginning." Together they all left that chamber, Kuli flying just above them as they ascended the stair.

Dinner was quite the performance, and Teresa was getting just a taste of what life at the Rookery had in store. While everyone was occupied trying to chase down runaway checker pieces, Daisy and Zora were able to sneak off to the study. Recreating the conditions to get down to the Observatory was difficult, but fortunately, Ms. Mizner had left her cane by the door, almost as if she knew they would need it right at that moment.

"Are you sure about this?" Daisy said, holding the cane above the seal on the floor.

"I am. This is how it should be," Zora replied. Together they opened the circular portal and descended into the Well of Memory.

Once they were inside the Observatory, they could see Orin was hard at work in his studies at the far end of the room.

"Hi Orin," Zora said, her voice echoing slightly through the space.

Orin looked up from his book, his stony face turning quickly into a broad smile. "Ms. Sparks? Ms. Kidd? What a pleasant surprise. It's lovely to see you both again."

Zora crossed the room until she stood in the rock giant's shadow. "I promised you I would introduce you to my friend," Zora said, and reached into her satchel, gently lifting Kuli out. "His name is Kuli. I figured he might stay here with you for a while and keep you company."

Kuli flew up to Orin and landed on the corner of his open book, letting out a chirp of greeting. "Hello friend," Orin replied and gently stroked the bird's coppery wings, "I'm delighted to meet you. I think you and I will be fast friends."

Zora turned to leave, but Orin spoke before she reached Daisy at the door. "You look different, Ms. Sparks, as if in the hours since last we saw one another you have grown."

Daisy gave her charge a measured look. "You know," she said, "he's got a point." Some how the stern young woman she had first met had a look in her eyes that could only be described as wisdom.

"I guess I have," she replied. "While we were at the gate, I saw something – just beyond the light. I can't be sure what it was, but I don't want to forget it. There is a whole other world out there, filled with secrets." Zora reached in her satchel and removed a small, glass mason jar. Inside, a dark mass twisted and turned like a tiny storm with flashes of green light.

"That's a piece of the Blade's weapon. You still have that?" Daisy asked, watching it along with Zora. "I'm pretty sure that stuff is dangerous to have around."

"Maybe, but we don't know. There is to much we don't know," Zora said, and returned the jar to her bag. "Somewhere out there is the power I need to help my mom, I know it in my heart, but there is still so much I have to learn."

Daisy wrapped her arm around Zora's shoulder. "Don't worry kiddo. I've got you're back," she said.

"Indeed, Ms. Kidd," Orin smiled. "We are all here to help you, Ms. Sparks." He looked around the Observatory. "Strange, but I think this place was built to help you. I, for one, am excited to begin."

Zora she was excited, too.

EPILOGUE:
MOUNT SHROUD

The halls of the Shroudhurst Psychiatric Hospital, even in the dead of night, were never quiet. There was a stillness that filled the space like a prevalent mist, sneaking into every nook and cranny, but never true silence. Every few moments you might hear one of the patients cry out, breaking the stillness with waking dreams, or maybe you would hear the tormented ramblings of another sitting by their door, conversing with people who weren't really there.

Tonight, the stillness was interrupted by a different sound. It started as a soft rush, like wind through an open window, that built to a roar in an instant, quickly subsiding. At the far end of the fifth ward hallway, a figure came into being, trailing shadows behind him like sand in a desert storm. By midway in the hall, he was fully formed, and the patients in each room could hear the resounding click of his heels on the tiled floor. As the figure passed one of those doors, a man looked out through the glass panel to see. The visitor was clad all in black, from his dark boots to his high-collared coat, and wore a strange mask with goggles, the head crested with dark feathers.

"You're not supposed to be here," the patient said, his voice trembling, "you're not supposed to be here."

The stranger did not speak but continued down the hall to his destination: the final room with A5 written above the glass viewing panel of the door. He stopped in front of it and peered in, then held his hand over the lock. A roil of darkness with bursts of green light formed and twisted into the keyhole, corroding it to dust.

The room was dark and sparse, but one high window opened to the world outside letting in thin trails of moonlight. As he walked inside, the stranger saw right away who he was looking for. A woman sat in the far corner, basking in the silver glow of the moon, her dark curls cascading down over her thin face. He stepped towards her, avoiding the light, instead crouching in the deep shadows just beyond.

"Do you know me?" he said, his voice echoing hollowly in that cold space.

She didn't answer. Laid out before where was an arrangement of cards, three across and two tall.

"Jennifer Sparks. Do. You. Know. Me?"

She looked up, turning over a card. It read The Warden. She stared at it for a minute, then looked up at him. "You are Raven," she said, but as if the words held very little meaning.

"Yes," Raven replied, his mask betraying no emotion. However, there was a relaxing of his shoulders when he heard her speak. "Do you know where your children are?"

Now the woman's expression changed quickly to fear. She turned over two more cards that read The Dagger and The Adept. "They are in danger. Terrible danger. "

"No. The danger has passed." Raven almost reached for her but knew better than to do so. There always those who were watching from beyond. "They are safe now," he said.

"Not safe," she said mournfully. She turned over another card, and this one read The Watcher. "The future is not safe."

Raven stood. "Then you know what I must do. The path has always been set – there is no turning back now." He turned and walked towards the dark corner of the room, fading like smoke with each step. "I will return, but until then, try to remember me." With that, he was gone.

Jennifer Sparks sat alone in her room, basking in a circle of moonlight, and a small smile appeared on her face. It was the first one she had in a long time.

"The future is not safe," she whispered, "but it's not set. Zora will change it." She picked up The Adept card and held it close, basking in the cool silver light. "She'll change everything."

THE RAVEN

ACKNOWLEDGEMENTS

Josie and I are people of faith – faith in wonder, in the basic goodness of others, and the continuing and benevolent force that guides our lives. Before we get to far into our thank yous, we want to thank God for getting us here, and never giving up on us. The path is laid before us, all we need do is walk it.

There are so many people that were instrumental in making this book a reality. As a small publishing company with big aspirations, their enthusiasm and kindness has been the spark that kept our creative lights aflame. *To our Kickstarter supporters* – thank you all for Believing In Wonder, and in us. *To our amazing editor, Rachel Lulich* – your guidance and skill are God sent. Please know that you are an indelible part of *The Wonderous Science*. *To Matt and Kesha Hawk, Buck Potter, and our 2nd Star Festival family* – you guys were there when this crazy experiment got started, and you've been an inspiration ever since. There is a little bit of the 2nd Star Festival in *The Wonderous Science*. *To Lisa Mantchez* – thank you for your kind words and encouragement. Having your support has elevated our book in so many ways. *To our proof-readers: Sean Fishback, Richard & Jaki Wolley, Margaret Schimming, and Ted Fauster* – you all are awesome and amazing people. Thank you so much for you help. *To the real Stephanie Love* – thank you for inspiring one of my favorite characters in this book. You are an incredible person. *To Jess Graff* – thank you for our time at Portland Children's Museum. It kept our spirits up (and our lights on) as we got Believe In Wonder off the ground. *To the Hammons Family* – in our time of struggle, you guys came through for us. We will always consider you not only our great friends, but also our family, our patrons, and our benefactors. *To Alethea and Gaytra* – thank you for taking a chance on us, your sound advice, and being in our corner. We hope this book leads to great things. *And to our family* – thank you for always believing in us, helping us through the tough times, and your constant prayers.

And a special thank you to our son, Victor Briant Parker – from the moment we heard your name, you have been our joy, and the greatest blessing that has ever been bestowed upon us. You inspire our stories everyday.

About the Creators of
THE WONDEROUS SCIENCE
& BELIEVE IN WONDER PUBLISHING

Brian W. Parker – AUTHOR, ILLUSTRATOR, and CREATOR OF THE FANTASTICAL

I grew up in Alaska, then Mississippi, and have always been in love with storytelling in every medium. Literature, movies, art, you name it! I have a BFA in graphic design and illustration, as well as a MA in writing and publishing, and worked as a graphic designer and illustrator for almost 15 years in music publishing, corporate marketing, and sports/entertainment.

Now I spend my days working on in youth publishing (so cool, right?) and teaching about the creative process. I'm always trying to learn and grow in my craft, and find that I am happiest when I'm striving to bring the works of my imagination to life, as well as sharing that experience with others. *Crow in the Hollow* is my first novel length work, but I have written ten picture books, and self published one graphic novel series titled YOU CAN RELY ON PLATYPI .

Josie A. Parker – CURATOR and ARTISAN OF IMAGINATION and WONDER

I grew up in the South, and I'm a southern girl at heart. My love of creativity has been lifelong, and is deeply rooted in my love for helping others. I've spent my adult life as a caregiver and paraprofessional with children and adults with special needs. My husband and I are also foster parents, and are strong advocates for children in the foster care system. Through my experiences, I've learned that I find great joy and inspiration in helping others find their own creative voices. Although I'm a poet and writer in my own right, I've found that I'm most happy in helping cultivate art within others, and guiding them through the ups and downs of the creative process .

Through Believe In Wonder , I bring to bear all of my experience to create classes and creative exploration events for children and young adults. I feel that by expanding our imaginations and our sense of wonder, we can achieve great things in our own lives, and help better the lives of others.

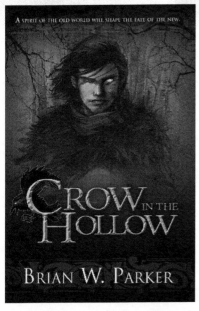

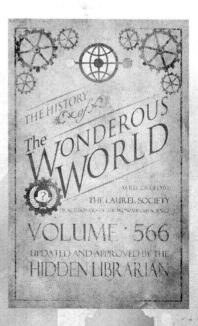